CASEY RYAN

People along Casey Ryan's Cripple Creek stage route said he drove the fastest six-horse rig in Colorado. Then the scrappy little Irishman with the pale blue squinty eyes graduated to a big Ford sedan carrying passengers (those who dared ride with him) through the Nevada desert, still refusing to turn aside for anything else on the road and bent on beating his own time. His acquisition of a marketable silver claim parlayed into an auto garage, an attractive widow's good cooking at a distant mine, a near fatal encounter with a mysterious, luring desert light and other peculiar developments lead Casey into enough trouble for three or four lifetimes.

CASEY RYAN

B. M. Bower

GUNSMOKE

First published by Hodder and Stoughton

This hardback edition 2003
by Chivers Press
by arrangement with
Golden West Literary Agency

Copyright © 1921 by B. M. Bower.
Copyright © 1922 by B. M. Bower in the
British Commonwealth.
Copyright © 1949 by Dele Newman Doke.
All rights reserved.

ISBN 0 7540 8230 X

British Library Cataloguing in Publication Data available.

London Borough of Barking & Dagenham	
VALENCE	
Askews	V
F	£9.95
001 076	937

Printed and bound in Great Britain by
Antony Rowe Ltd., Chippenham, Wiltshire

CASEY RYAN

CHAPTER I

From Denver to Spokane, from El Paso to Fort Benton, men talk of Casey Ryan and smile when they speak his name. Old men with the flat tone of coming senility in their voices will suck at their pipes and cackle reminiscently while they tell you of Casey's tumultuous youth — when he drove the six fastest horses in Colorado on the stage out from Cripple Creek, and whooped past would-be holdups with a grin of derision on his face and bullets whining after him and passengers praying disjointed prayers and clinging white-knuckled to the seats.

They say that once a flat, lanky man climbed bareheaded out at the stage station below the mountain and met Casey coming springily off the box with whip and six reins in his hand. The lanky man was still pale from his ride, and he spluttered when he spoke:

"Sa-ay! N-next time you're held up and I'm r-ridin' with yuh, b-by gosh, you s-*stop*. I-I'd ruther be shot t-than p-pitched off into a c-canyon s-somewhere a-and busted up!"

Casey is a little man. When he was young he was slim, but he always has owned a pale blue, unwinking squint which he uses with effect. He halted where he was and squinted up at the man, and spat fluid tobacco and grinned.

"You're here, and you're able to kick about my drivin'. That's purty good luck, I'd say. You *ain't* shot, an' you ain't layin' busted in no canyon. Any time a man gits shot outa Casey Ryan's stage, he'll have to jump out an' wait for the bullet to ketch up. And there ain't any passengers offn' this stage layin' busted in no canyon, neither. I bring in what I start out with."

The other man snorted and reached under his coat tail for the solacing plug of chewing tobacco. Opposition and ridicule had brought a little color into his face.

"Why, hell, man! You — you come around that ha-hairpin turn up there on two wheels! It's a miracle we wasn't —"

"Miracles is what happens once and lets it go at that. Say! Casey Ryan *always* saves wear on a coupla wheels, on that turn. I've made it on one; but the leaders wasn't runnin' right to-day. That nigh one's cast a shoe. I gotta have that looked after." He gave up the reins to the waiting hostler and went off, heading straight for the station porch where waited a red-haired girl with freckles and a warm smile for Casey.

That was Casey's youth; part of it. The rest was made up of fighting, gambling, drinking hilariously with the crowd and always with his temper on hair trigger. Along the years behind him he left a straggling procession of men, women and events. The men and women would always know the color of his eyes and would recognize the Casey laugh in a crowd, years after they had last heard it; the events were full of the true Casey flavor,— and as I say, when men told of them and mentioned Casey, they laughed.

From the time when his daily drives were likely to be interrupted by holdups, and once by a grizzly that reared up in the road fairly under the nose of his leaders and sent the stage off at an acute angle, blazing a trail by itself amongst the timber, Casey drifted from mountain to desert, from desert to plain and back again, blithely meeting hard luck face to face and giving it good day as if it were a friend. For Casey was born an optimist, and misfortune never quite got him down and kept him there, though it tried hard and often, as you will presently see. Some called him gritty. Some said he hadn't the sense to know when he was licked. Either way, it made a rare little Irishman of Casey Ryan, and kept his name from becoming blurred in the memories of those who once knew him.

So in time it happened that Casey was driving a stage of his own from Pinnacle down to Lund, in Nevada, and making boast that his four horses could beat the record — the month's record, mind — of any dog-gone auty-*mo*-bile that ever infested the trail. Infest is a word that Casey would have used often had he known its dictionary reputation. Having been deprived of close acquaintance with dictionaries, but having a facile imagination and some creative ability, Casey kept pace with progress and invented words of his own which he applied lavishly to all automobiles; but particularly and emphatically he applied the spiciest, most colorful ones to Fords.

Put yourself in Casey's place, and you will understand. Imagine yourself with a thirty-mile trip to make down a twisty, rough mountain road built in the days when men hauled ore down the mountain on wagons built to bump over rocks without damage to anything but human bones. You are Casey Ryan, remember; you never stopped for stage robbers or grizzlies in the past, and you have your record to maintain as the hardest driver in the West. You are proud of that record, because you know how you have driven to earn it.

You pop the lash over the ears of your leaders and go whooping down a long, straight bit of road where you count on making time. When you are about halfway down and the four horses are running even and tugging pleasantly at the reins, and you are happy enough to sing your favorite song, which begins,

"Hey, ole Bill! Can-n yuh play the fiddle-o?
Yes, by gosh! I — I — kin play a liddle-o —"

and never gets beyond that one flat statement, around the turn below you comes a Ford, rattling all its joints trying to make the hill on " high." The driver honks wildly at you to give him the road — you, Casey Ryan! Wouldn't you writhe and invent words and apply them viciously to all Fords and the man who invented them? But the driver comes at you honking, squawking,— and you turn out.

You have to, unless the Ford does; and Fords don't. A Ford will send a twin-six swerving sharply to the edge of a ditch, and even Casey Ryan must swing his leaders to the right in obedience to that raucous command.

Once Casey didn't. He had the patience of the good-natured, and for awhile he had contented himself with his vocabulary and his reputation as a driver and a fighter, and the record he held of making the thirty miles from Pinnacle to Lund in an hour and thirty-five minutes, twenty-six days in the month. (He did not publish his running expenses, by the way, nor did he mention the fact that his passengers were mostly strangers picked up at the railway station at Lund because they liked the look of the picturesque four-horses-and-Casey stage-coach.)

Once Casey refused to turn out. That morning he had been compelled to wait and whip a heavy man who berated Casey because the heavy man's wife had ridden from Pinnacle to Lund the day before and had fainted at the last sharp turn in the road and had not revived in time to board the train for Salt Lake which she had been anxious to catch. Casey had known she was anxious to catch the train, and he had made the trip in an hour and twenty-nine minutes in spite of the fact that he had driven the last mile with a completely unconscious lady leaning heavily against his left shoulder. She made much better time with Casey than she would have made on the narrow-gauge train which carried ore and passengers and mail to Lund, arriving when most convenient to the train crew. That it took half an hour to restore her to consciousness was not Casey's fault.

Casey had succeeded in whipping the heavy man till he hollered, but the effort had been noticeable. Casey wondered uneasily whether by any chance he, Casey Ryan, was growing old with the rest of the world. That possibility had never before occurred to him, and the thought was disquieting. Casey Ryan too old to lick any man who gave him cause, too old to hold the fickle esteem of those who met him in the road? Casey squinted belligerently at the Old-man-with-the-scythe and snorted. "I licked him good. You ask anybody. And he's twice as big as I am. I guess they's a good many years left in Casey Ryan yet! Giddap, you — thus-and-so! We're ten minutes late and we got our record!"

At that moment a Ford touring car popped around the turn below him and squawked presumptuously for a clear passage ahead. Casey pulled his lash off the nigh leader, yelled and charged straight down the road. Did they think they could honk him off the road? Hunh! Casey Ryan was still Casey Ryan. Never again would he turn out for man or devil.

Wherefore Casey was presently extricating his leaders from the harness of his wheelers ten feet below the grade. On the road above him the driver of the Ford inspected bent parts and a smashed headlight and cranked and cranked ineffectively, and swore down at Casey Ryan, who squinted unblinkingly up under his hatbrim at the man he likewise cussed.

They were a long while there exchanging disagreeable opinions of one another, and Casey was even obliged to climb the steep bank and whip the driver of the Ford because he had applied a word to Casey which had never failed as automatic prelude to a Casey Ryan combat. Casey was frankly winded when he finally mounted one of his horses and led the other three, and so proceeded to Lund as mad as he had ever been in his life.

"That there settles it final," he snorted, when the town came into view in the flat below. "They've pushed Casey off'n the grade for the first time and the last time. What pushin' and crowdin' and squawkin' is done from now on, it'll be Casey Ryan doin' it! Faint! I'll learn 'em something to faint about. If it's Fords goin' to run horses off'n the trail, you watch how Casey Ryan'll drive the livin' tar outa one. Dog-gone 'em, there ain't no Ford livin' that can drive Casey off'n the road. I'll drive 'em till their tongues hang out. I'll make 'em bawl like a calf, and I'll pound 'em on the back and make 'em fan it faster."

So talking to himself and his team he rode into town and up to one of those ubiquitous Ford agencies that write their curly-tailed blue lettering across the continent from the high nose of Maine to the shoulder of Cape Flattery.

"Gimme one of them dog-goned blankety bing-bing Ford auty-*mo*-biles," he commanded the garage owner who came to meet Casey amiably in his shirt sleeves. "Here's four horses I'll trade yuh, with what's left of the harness. And up at the third turn you'll find a good wheel off'n the stage." He slid down from the sweaty back of his nigh leader and stood slightly bow-legged and very determined before the garage owner, Bill Masters.

"Wel-l — there ain't much sale for horses, Casey. I ain't got any place to keep 'em, nor any feed. I'll sell yuh a Ford on time, and —"

Casey glanced over his shoulder to make sure the horses were standing quiet, dropped the reins and advanced upon Bill.

"You *trade*," he stated flatly.

Bill backed a little. "Oh, all right, if that's the way yuh feel. What yuh askin' for the four just as they stand?"

"Me? A Ford auty-*mo*-bile. I told yuh that, Bill. And I want you to put on the biggest horn that's made; one that can be heard from here to Pinnacle and back when I turn 'er loose. And run the damn thing out here right away and show me how it works, and how often you gotta wind it and when. Lucky I didn't bring no passengers down — I was runnin' empty. But I gotta take back a load of Bohunks to the Bluebird this afternoon, and my stage, she's a total wreck. I'll sign papers to-night if you got any to sign."

CHAPTER II

Thus was the trade effected with much speed and few preliminaries, because Bill knew Casey Ryan very intimately and had seen him in action when his temper was up. Bill adjusted an extra horn which he happened to have in stock. One of those terrific things that go far toward making the life of a pedestrian a nerve-racking succession of startles. Casey tried it out on himself before he would accept it. He walked several doors down the street with the understanding that Bill would honk at him when he was some little distance away. Bill waited until Casey's attention was drawn to a lady with thick ankles who was crossing the street in a hurry and a stiff breeze. Bill came down on the metal plunger of the horn with all his might, and Casey jumped perceptibly and came back grinning.

" She'll do. What'll put a crimp in Casey Ryan's spine is good enough for anybody. Bring her out here and show me how yuh work the damn thing. Guess she'll hold six Bohunks, won't she — with sideboards on? I'll run 'er around a coupla times b'fore I start out — and that's all I will do."

Naturally the garage man was somewhat perturbed at this nonchalant manner of getting acquainted with a Ford. He knew the road from Lund to Pinnacle. He had driven it himself, with

There were chatterings and gesticulations in the tonneau. Out of the gabble a shrill voice rose beseechingly in English. "We will *walk,* meester! If you *pleese,* meester! We are 'fraid for ride wit' dees may*chine,* meester!"

Casey was nettled by the cackling and the thigh-slapping of the audience on the sidewalk. He reached for his stage whip, and missing it used his ready Irish fists. So the Bohunks crawled unhappily back into the car and subsided shivering and with tears in their eyes.

"Dammit, when I take on passengers to ride, they're goin' to *ride* till they git there. You shut up, back there!"

A friend of Casey's stepped forward and cranked the machine, and Casey pulled down the gas lever until the motor howled, turned in the shortest possible radius and went lunging up the crooked steep trail to the Bluebird mine on top of the hill, his engine racing and screaming in low.

Thereafter Pinnacle and Lund had a new standard by which to measure the courage of a man. Had he made the trip with Casey Ryan and his new Ford? He *had?* By golly, he sure had nerve. One man passed the peak for sheer bravery and rode twice with Casey, but certain others were inclined to disparage the feat, on the ground that on the second trip he was drunk.

Casey did not like that. He admitted that he was a hard driver; he had always been proud because men called him the hardest driver in the West. But he argued that he was also a safe driver, and that they had no business to make such a fuss over riding with him. Didn't he ride after his own driving every day of his life? Had he ever got killed? Had he ever killed anybody else? Well! What were they all yawping about, then? Pinnacle and Lund made him tired.

"If you fellers think I can't bounce that there tin can down the road fast as any man in the country, why don't yuh pass me on the road? You're welcome. Just try it."

No one cared to try, however. Meeting him was sufficiently hazardous. There were those who secretly timed their traveling so that they would not see Casey Ryan at all, and I don't think you can really call them cowards, either. A good many had families, you know.

Casey had an accident now and then; and his tire expense was such as to keep him up nights playing poker for money to support his Ford. You simply can't whirl into town at a thirty-mile gait — I am speaking now of Pinnacle, whose street was a gravelly creek bed quite dry and ridgy between rains — and stop in twice the car's length without scouring more rubber off your tires than a capacity load of passengers will pay for. Besides, you run short of passengers if you persist in doing it. Even the strangers who came in on the Salt Lake line were quite likely to look once at the cute little narrow-gauge train with its cunning little day coach hitched behind a string of ore cars, glance at Casey's Ford stage with indifference and climb into the cunning day coach for the trip to Pinnacle. The psychology of it passed quite over Casey's head, but his pocket felt the change.

In two weeks — perhaps it was less, though I want to be perfectly just — Casey was back, afoot and standing bow-legged in the doorway of Bill Master's garage at Lund.

"Gimme another one of them Ford auty-*mo*-biles," he requested, grinning a little. "I guess mebby I oughta take two or three — but I'm a little short right now, Bill. I ain't been gitting any good luck at poker, lately."

Bill asked a question or two while he led Casey to the latest model of Fords, just in from the factory.

Casey took a chew of tobacco and explained. "Well, I had a bet up, y'see. That red-headed bartender in Pinnacle bet me a hundred dollars I couldn't beat my own record ten minutes on the trip down. I knowed I could, so I took him up on it. A man would be a fool if he didn't grab any easy money like that. And so I pounded 'er on the tail, coming down. And I had eight minutes peeled off my best time, and then Jim Black he had to go git in the road on that last turn up there. We rammed our noses together and I pushed him on ahead of me for fifty rods, Bill — and him yelling at me to quit — but something busted in the insides of my car, I guess. She give a grunt and quit. All right, I'll take this one. Grease her up, Bill. I'll eat a bite before I take her up."

You've no doubt suspected before now that not even poker, played industriously o' nights, could

CASEY RYAN 15

keep Casey's head above the financial waters that threatened to drown him and his Ford and his reputation. Casey did not mind repair bills, so long as he achieved the speed he wanted. But he did mind not being able to pay the repair bills when they were presented to him. Whatever else were his faults, Casey Ryan had always gone cheerfully into his pocket and paid what he owed. Now he was haunted by a growing fear that an unlucky game or two would send him under, and that he might not come up again.

He began to think seriously of selling his car and going back to horses which, in spite of the high cost of feeding them, had paid their way and his, and left him a pleasant jingle in his pockets. But then he bumped hard into one of those queer little psychological facts which men never take into account until it is too late. Casey Ryan, who had driven horses since he could stand on his toes and fling harness on their backs, could not go back to driving horses. The speed fiend of progress had him by the neck. Horses were too slow for Casey. Moreover, when he began to think about it, he knew that the thirty-mile stretch between Pinnacle and Lund had become too tame for him, too monotonous. He knew in the dark every twist in the road, every sharp turn, and he could tell you offhand what every sharp turn had cost him in the past month, either in repairs to his own car or to the car that had unluckily met him without warning. For Casey, I must tell you, habitually forgot all about that ear-splitting klaxon at his left elbow. He was always in too much of a hurry to blow it; and anyway, by the time he reached a turn, he was around it; there either was no car in the road or Casey had scraped paint off it or worse and gone on. So why honk?

Far distances called Casey. In one day, he meditated, he could cover more desert with his Ford than horses could travel in a week. An old, half-buried passion stirred, lifted its head and smiled at him seductively,— a dream he had dreamed of finding some of that wealth which Nature holds so miser-like in her hills. A gold mine, or perhaps silver or copper,— what matter which mineral he found, so long as it spelled wealth for him? Then he would buy a bigger car and a faster car, and he would bore farther and farther into yonder. In his past were tucked away months on end of tramping across deserts and up mountain defiles with a packed burro nipping patiently along in front of him and this same, seductive dream beckoning him over the next horizon. Burros had been slow. While he hurtled down the road from Pinnacle to Lund, Casey pictured himself plodding through sand and sage and over malapai and up dry canyons, hazing a burro before him.

"No, sir, the time for that is gone by. I could do in a week now what it took me a month to do then. I could get into country a man'd hate to tackle afoot, not knowing the water holes. I'll git me a radiator that don't boil like a teakettle over a pitch fire, and load up with water and grub and gas, and I'll find the Injun Jim mine, mebby. Or some other darn mine that'll put me in the clear the rest

CASEY RYAN 17

of my life. Couldn't before, because I had to travel too slow. But shucks! A Ford can go anywhere a mountain goat can go. You ask anybody."

So Casey sold his stage line and the hypothetical good will that went with it, and Pinnacle and Lund breathed long and deep and planned trips they had refrained from taking heretofore, and wished Casey luck. Bill Masters laid a friendly hand on his shoulder and made a suggestion so wise that not even Casey could shut his mind against it.

"You're starting out where there won't be no Bill handy to fix what you bust," he pointed out. "You wait over a day or two, Casey, and let me show yuh a few things about that car. If you bust down on the desert you'll want to know what's wrong, and how to fix it. It's easy, but you got to know where to look for the trouble."

"Me? Say, Bill, I never had to go lookin' for trouble," Casey grinned. "What do I need to learn how for?"

Nevertheless he remained all of that day with Bill and crammed on mechanics. He was amazed to discover how many and how different were the ailments that might afflict a Ford. That he had boldly — albeit unconsciously — driven a thing filled with timers, high-tension plugs that may become fouled and fail to "spark," carburetors that could get out of adjustment (whatever that was) spark plugs that burned out and had to be replaced, a transmission that absolutely *must* have grease or something happened, bearings that were prone to burn out if they went dry of oil, and a multitude of other mishaps that could happen and did happen if one did not watch out, would have filled Casey with foreboding if that were possible. Being an optimist to the middle of his bones, he merely felt a growing pride in himself. He had actually driven all this aggregation of potential internal grief! Whenever anything had happened to his Ford *auty-mo*-bile between Pinnacle and Lund, Casey never failed to trace the direct cause, which had always been external rather than internal, save that time when he had walked in and bought a new car without probing into the vitals of the other.

"I'd ruther have a horse down with glanders," he sighed, when Bill finally washed the grease off his hands and forearms and rolled down his sleeves. "But Casey Ryan's game to try anything once, and most things the second and third time. You ask anybody. Gimme all the hootin'-annies that's liable to wear out, Bill, and a load uh tires and patches, and Casey'll come back and hand yuh a diamond big as your fist, some day. Ole Lady Trouble's always tryin' to take a fall outa me, but she's never got me down so't I had to holler 'nough. You ask anybody. Casey Ryan's goin' out to see what he can see. If he meets up with Miss Fortune, he'll tame her, Bill. And this little Ford auty-*mo*-bile is goin' to eat outa my hand. I don't give a cuss if she does git sore and ram her spark plugs into her carburetor now and agin. She'll know who's boss, Bill. I learnt it to the burros, and what you can learn a burro you can learn a Ford, take time enough."

Taking that point of view and keeping it, Casey managed very well. Whenever anything went wrong that his vocabulary and a monkey wrench could not mend, Casey sat down on the shadiest running board and conned the Instruction Book which Bill handed him at the last minute. Other times he treated the Ford exactly as he would treat a burro, with satisfactory results.

CHAPTER III

Away out on the high mesas that are much like the desert below, except that the nights are cool and the wind is not fanned out of a furnace, Casey fought sand and brush and rocks and found a trail now and then which he followed thankfully, and so came at last to a short range of mountains whose name matched well their inhospitable stare. The Starvation Mountains had always been reputed rich in mineral and malevolent in their attitude toward man and beast. Even the Joshua trees stood afar off and lifted grotesque arms defensively against them. But Casey was not easily daunted, and eerie places held for him no meaning save the purely material one. If he could find water and the rich vein of ore some one had told him was there, then Casey would be happy in spite of snakes, tarantulas and sinister stories of the place.

Water he found, not too far up a gulch. So he pitched his tent within carrying distance from the spring, thanked the god of mechanics that an automobile neither eats nor drinks when it does not work, and set out to find his fortune.

Casey knew there was a mining camp on the high slope of Barren Butte. He knew the name of the camp, which was Lucky Lode, and he knew the foreman there — knew him from long ago in the days when Casey was what he himself confessed to be wild. In reaching Starvation Mountains, Casey had driven for fifteen miles within plain sight of Lucky Lode. But gas is precious when you are a hundred miles from a garage, and since business did not take him there Casey did not drive up the five-mile hill to the Lucky Lode just to shake hands with the foreman and swap a yarn or two. Instead, he headed down on to the bleached, bleak oval of Furnace Lake and forged across it as straight as he could drive toward Starvation Mountains.

But the next time Casey made the trip — needing supplies, powder, fuse, caps and so on — Fate took him by the ear and led him to a lady. This is how Fate did it,— and I will say it was an original idea:

Casey had a gallon syrup can in the car which he used for extra oil for the engine. Having an appetite for sour-dough biscuits and syrup, he had also a gallon can of syrup in the car. It was a terrifically hot day, and the wind that biew full against Casey's left cheek as he drove burned even his leather skin where it struck. Casey was afraid he was running short of water, and a Ford's comfort comes first,— as every man knows; so that Casey was parched pretty thoroughly, inside and out. Within a mile of Furnace Lake he stopped, took an unsatisfying sip from his big canteen and emptied the rest of the water into the radiator. Then he replenished the oil in the motor generously, cranked and went bumping along down the trail worn rough with the trucks from Lucky Lode.

For a little way he jounced along the trail; then

the motor began to labor; and although Casey pulled the gas lever down as far as it would go, the car slowed and stopped dead in the road. After an hour of fruitless monkey-wrenching and swearing and sweating, Casey began to suspect something. He examined both cans, "hefted" them, smelt and even tasted the one half-empty, and decided that Ford auty-*mo*-biles do not require two quarts of syrup at one dose. He thought that a little syrup ought not to make much difference, but half a gallon was probably too much.

He put in more oil on top of the syrup, but he could not even move the crank, much less "turn 'er over." So long as a man can wind the crank of a Ford he seems able to keep alive his hopes. Casey could not crank, wherefore he knew himself beaten even while he heaved and lifted and swore, and strained every muscle in his back lifting again. He got so desperately wrathful that he lifted the car perceptibly off its right front wheel with every heave, but he felt as if he were trying to lift a boulder.

It was past supper time at Lucky Lode when Casey arrived, staggering a little with exhaustion, both mental and physical. His eyes were bloodshot with the hot wind, his face was purple from the same wind, his lips were dry and rough. I cannot blame the men at Lucky Lode for a sudden thirst when they saw him coming, and a hope that he still had a little left. And when he told them that he had filled his engine with syrup instead of oil, what would any one think?

Their unjust suspicions would not have worried

Casey in the least, had Lucky Lode not possessed a lady cook who was a lady. She was a widow with two children, and she had the children with her and held herself aloof from the men in a manner befitting a lady. Casey was hungry and thirsty and tired, and, as much as was possible to his nature, disgusted with life in general. The widow gave him a smile of sympathy which went straight to his heart, and hot biscuits and coffee and beans cooked the way he liked them best. These went straight to ease the gnawing emptiness of his stomach, and being a man who took his emotions at their face value, he jumped to the conclusion that it was the lady whose presence gave him the glow.

Casey stayed that night and the next day and the next at Lucky Lode. The foreman helped him tow the syruppy car up the hill to the machine shop where he could get at it, and Casey worked until night trying to remove the dingbats from the hootin'-annies,— otherwise, the pistons from the cylinders. The foreman showed him what to do, and Casey did it, using a "double-jack" and a lot of energy.

Before he left the Lucky Lode, Casey knew exactly what syrup will do to a Ford if applied internally, and the widow had promised to marry him if he would stop drinking and smoking and swearing. Since Casey had not been drunk in ten years on account of having seen a big yellow snake with a green head on the occasion of his last carouse, he took the drinking pledge quite cheerfully for her sake. He promised to stop smoking, glad that the widow neglected to mention chewing tobacco, which was his

CHAPTER IV

Being Casey Ryan, tough as hickory and wont to drive headlong to his destination, Casey did not remain in town to loiter a half a day and sleep a night and drive back the next day, as most desert dwellers did. He hurried through with his business, filled up with gas and oil, loaded on an extra can of each, strapped his box of dynamite upon the seat beside him where he could keep an eye on it — just as if that would do any good if the tricky stuff meant to blow up! — and started back at three in the afternoon. He would be half the night getting to camp, even though he was Casey Ryan and drove a mean Ford. But he would be there, ready to start work at sunrise. A man who is going to marry a widow with two children had best hurry up and strike every streak of rich ore he has in his claim, thought Casey.

All that afternoon, though the wind blew hot in his face, Casey drilled across the desert, meeting never a living thing, overtaking none. All that afternoon a yellow dust cloud swirled rapidly along the rough desert road, vainly trying to keep up with Casey who made it. In Yucca Pass he had to stop and fill motor and radiator with oil and water, and just as he topped the summit a front tire popped like a pistol.

Casey killed the engine and got out a bit stiffly,

CASEY RYAN

pried off a chew of tobacco and gazed pensively at Barren Butte that held Lucky Lode, where the widow was cooking supper at that moment. Casey wished practically that he was there and could sit down to some of her culinary achievements.

"I sure would like to flop m' lip over one of her biscuits right now," he said aloud. "If I do strike it, I wonder will she git too high-toned to cook?"

His eyes went to Furnace Lake, lying smooth and pale yellow in the saucerlike basin between Barren Butte and the foothills of Starvation. In the soft light of the afterglow it seemed to smile at him with a glint of malice, like the treacherous thing it was. For Furnace Lake is treacherous. The Big Earthquake (America knows only one Big Earthquake, that which rocked San Francisco so disastrously) had split Furnace Lake halfway across, leaving an ugly crevice ten feet wide at the narrowest point and eighty feet deep, men said. Time and passing storms had partly filled the gash, but it was there, ugly, ominous, a warning to all men to trust the lake not at all. Little cracks radiated from the big gash here and there, and the cattle men rode often that way, though not often enough to save their cattle from falling in.

By day the lake shimmered deceptively with mirages that painted it blue with the likeness of water. Then a lone clump of greasewood stood up tall and proclaimed itself a ship lying idle on a glassy expanse of water so blue, so cool, so clear, one could not wonder that thirsty travelers went mad sometimes with the false lure of it.

Just now the lake looked exactly like any lake at dusk, with the far shore line reflected along its edge; and Casey's thought went beyond, to his claim on Starvation. Being tired and hungry, he pictured wistfully a cabin there, and a light in the window when he went chuckling up the long mesa in the dark, and the widow inside with hot coffee and supper waiting for him. Just as soon as he struck "shipping values" that picture would be real, said Casey to himself; and he opened his tool box and set to work changing the tire.

By the time he had finished it was dark, and Casey had yet a long forty miles between himself and his sour-dough can. He cranked the engine, switched on the electric headlights, and went tearing down the fifteen-mile incline to the lake.

"She c'n see the lights, and she'll know I ain't hangin' out in town lappin' up whisky," he told himself as he drove. "She'll know it's Casey Ryan comin' home — know it the way them lights are slippin' over the country. Ain't another man on the desert can put a car over the trail like this! You ask anybody."

Pleased with himself and his reputation, urged by hunger and the desire to make good on his claim so that he might have the little home he instinctively craved, Casey pulled the gas lever down another eighth of an inch — when he was already using more than he should — and nearly bounced his dynamite off the seat when he lurched over a sandy hummock and down on to the smooth floor of the lake.

It was five miles across that lake from rim to rim and taking a straight line, as Casey did, well above the crevice. In all that distance there is not a stick, or a stone, or a bush to mark the way. Not even a trail, since Casey was the only man who traveled it, and Casey never made tracks twice in the same place, but drove down upon it, picked himself a landmark on the opposite side and steered for it exactly as one steers a boat. The marks he left behind him were no more than pencil marks drawn upon a sheet of buff wrapping paper. Unless the lake was wet with one of those sporadic desert rains, you couldn't make any impression on the cement-like surface.

And when the lake was wet, you stuck where you were until wind and sun dried it for you. Wherefore Casey plunged out upon five miles of blank, baked clay with neither road, chart nor compass to guide him. It was the first time he had ever crossed at night, and a blanket of thin, high clouds hid the stars.

Casey thought nothing much of that,— being Casey Ryan. He had before him the dim — very dim — outline of Starvation, and being perfectly sober, he steered a straight course, and made sure he was well away from the upper end of the crevice, and pulled the gas lever down another notch.

The little handful of engine roared beautifully and shook the car with the vibration. Casey heaved a sigh of weariness mingled with content that the way was smooth and he need not look for chuck holes for a few minutes, at any rate. He settled back, and his fingers relaxed on the wheel. I think he dozed, though Casey swears he did not.

Suddenly he leaned forward, stared hard, leaned out and stared, listened with an ear cocked toward the engine. He turned and looked behind, then stared ahead again.

"By *gosh,* I bet both hubs is busted!" he ejaculated under his breath,— Furnace Lake subdues one somehow. "She's runnin' like a wolf — but she ain't goin'!"

He waited for a minute longer, trifling with the gas, staring and listening. The car was shaking with the throb of the motor, but Casey could feel no forward motion. "Settin' here burnin' gas like a 'lection bonfire — she sure *would* think I'm drunk if she knowed it," Casey muttered, and straddled over the side of the car to the running board.

"I wish — to — *hell* I hadn't promised her not to cuss!" he gritted, and with one hand still on the wheel, Casey shut off the gas and stepped down.

He stepped down upon a surface sliding beneath him at the rate of close to forty miles an hour. The Ford went on, spinning away from him in a wide circle, since Casey had unconsciously turned the wheel to the left as he let go. The blow of meeting the hard clay stunned him just at first, and he had rolled over a couple of times before he began to regain his senses.

He lifted himself groggily to his knees and looked for the car, saw it bearing down upon him from the direction whence he had come. Before he had time to wonder much at the phenomenon, it was upon him, over with a lurch, and gone again.

Casey was tough, and he never knew when he was whipped. He crawled up to his knees again, saw the same Ford coming at him with dimming headlights from the same direction it had taken before, made a wild grab for it, was knocked down and run over again. You may not believe that, but Casey had the bruises to prove it.

On the third round the Ford had slowed to a walk, figuratively speaking. Casey was pretty dizzy, and he thought his back was broken, but he was mad clear through. He caught the Ford by its fender, hung on, clutching frantically for a better hold, was dragged a little distance so and then, as its speed slackened to a gentle forward roll, he made shift to get aboard and give the engine gas before it had quite stopped. Which he told himself was lucky, because he couldn't have cranked the thing to save his life.

By sheer, dogged nerve he drove to camp, drank cold coffee left from his early breakfast, and decided that the bite of a Ford, while it is poisonous, is not necessarily fatal unless it attacks one in a vital spot.

Casey could not drill a hole, he could not swing a pick; for two days he limped groaning around camp and confined his activities to cooking his meals. Frequently he would look at the Ford and shake his head. There was something uncanny about it.

"She sure has got it in for me," he mused. "You can't blame her for runnin' off when I dropped the reins and stepped out. But that don't account for the way she come *at* me, and the way she *got* me every circle she made. That's human. It's dog-*gone* human! I've cussed her a lot, and I've done things to her — like that syrup I poured into her — and dog-gone her, she's been layin' low and watchin' her chance all this while. Fords, I believe, are about as human as horses, and I've knowed horses I believe coulda talked if their tongues was split. Ask anybody.. That there car *knowed!*"

The third day after the attack Casey was still too sore to work, but he managed to crank the Ford — eyeing it curiously the while, and with respect, too — and started down the mesa and up over the ridge and on down to the lake. He was still studying the matter incredulously, still wondering if Fords can think. He wanted to tell the widow about it and get her opinion. The widow was a smart woman. A little touchy on the liquor question, maybe, but smart. You ask anybody.

Lucky Lode greeted him with dropped jaws and wide staring eyes, which puzzled Casey until the foreman, grasping his shoulder — which made Casey wince and break a promise — explained their astonishment. They had, as Casey expected, seen his lights when he came off the summit from Yucca Pass. By the speed they traveled, Lucky Lode knew that Casey and no other was at the steering wheel, even before he took to the lake.

"And then," said the foreman, "we saw your lights go round and round in a circle, and disappear —"

"They didn't," Casey cut in trenchantly. "They went dim because I was taking her slow, being about all in."

The foreman grinned. "We thought you'd drove into the crevice, and we went down with lanterns and hunted the full length of it. We never found a sign of you or the car —"

"'Cause I was over in camp, or thereabouts," interpolated Casey drily. "I wish you'd of come on over. I sure needed help."

"We figured you was pretty well lit up, to circle around like that. I've been down since, by daylight, and so have some of the boys, looking into that crevice. But we gave it up, finally."

Then Casey, because he liked a joke even when it was on himself, told the foreman and his men what had happened to him. He did not exaggerate the mishap; the truth was sufficiently wild.

They whooped with glee. Every one laughs at the unusual misfortunes of others, and this was unusual. They stood around the Ford and talked to it, and whooped again. "You sure must have had so-ome jag, Casey," they told him exuberantly.

"I was sober," Casey testified earnestly. "I'll swear I hadn't a drop of anything worse than lemon soda, and that was before I left town." Whereupon they whooped the louder, bent double, some of them with mirth.

"Say! If I was drunk that night, I'd say so," Casey exploded finally. "What the hell — what's the matter with you rabbits? You think Casey Ryan has got to the point where he's scared to tell what he done and all he done? Lemme tell yuh, anything Casey does he ain't afraid to *tell* about! Lyin' is something I never was scared bad enough to do. You ask anybody."

"There's the widow," said the foreman, wiping his eyes.

Casey turned and looked, but the widow was not in sight. The foreman, he judged, was speaking figuratively. He swung back glaring.

"You think I'm scared to tell her what happened? She'll know I was sober if I say I was sober. She ain't as big a fool—" He did not want to fight, although he was aching to lick every man of them. But for one thing, he was too sore and lame, and then, the widow would not like it.

With his neck very stiff, Casey limped down to the house and tried to tell the widow. But the widow was a woman, and she was hurt because Casey, since he was alive and not in the crevice, had not come straight to comfort her, but had lingered up there talking and laughing with the men. The widow had taken Casey's part when the others said he must have been drunk. She had maintained, red-lidded and trembly of voice, that something had gone wrong with Casey's car so that he couldn't steer it. Such things happened, she knew.

Well, Casey told the widow the truth, and the widow's face hardened while she listened. She had permitted him to kiss her when he came in, but now she moved away from him. She did not call him dear boy, nor even Casey dear. She waited until he had reached the point that puzzled him, the point

CASEY RYAN

of a Ford's degree of intelligence. Then her lips thinned before she opened them.

"And what," she asked coldly, "had you been drinking, Mr. Ryan?"

"Me? One bottle of lemon soda before I left town, and I left town at three o'clock in the afternoon. I swear —"

"You need not swear, Mr. Ryan." The widow folded her hands and regarded him sternly, though her voice was still politely soft. "After I had told you repeatedly that my little ones should ever be guarded from a drinking father; after you had solemnly promised me that you would never again put glass to your lips, or swallow a drop of whisky; after that very morning renewing your pledge —"

"Well, I kept it," Casey said, his face a shade paler under its usual frank red. "I swear to Gawd I was sober."

"You need not lie," said the widow, "and add to your misdeeds. You were drunk. No man in his senses would imagine what you imagine, or do what you did. I wish you to understand, Mr. Ryan, that I shall not marry you. I could not trust you out of my sight."

"I — was — *sober!*" cried Casey, measuring his words. Very nearly shouting them, in fact.

The widow turned pointedly away and began to stir something on the stove, and did not look at him.

Casey went out, climbed the hill to his Ford, cranked it and went larruping down the hill, out on the lake and, when he had traversed half its length, turned and steered a straight course across it.

Where tracings of wheels described a wide circle he stopped and regarded them intently. Then he began to swear, at nothing in particular, but with a hearty enjoyment of the phrases he intoned.

"Casey, you sure as hell have had one close call," he remarked, when he could think of nothing new and devilish to say. "You mighta run along, and run along, till you got *married* to her. Whadda I want a wife for, anyway? Sour-dough biscuits tastes pretty good, and Casey sure can make 'em!" He got out his pipe, filled it and crammed down the tobacco, found a match and leaned back, smoking with relish, one leg thrown over the wheel.

"A man's best friend is his Ford," he exclaimed. "You can ask anybody." He grinned, and blew a lot of smoke, and gave the wheel an affectionate little twist.

CHAPTER V

Some months later Casey waved good-by to the men from Tonopah, squinted up at the sun and got a coal-oil can of water, with which he filled the radiator of his Ford. He rolled his bed in the tarp and tied it securely, put flour, bacon, coffee, salt and various other small necessities of life into a box, inspected his sour-dough can, and decided to empty it and start over again if hard fate drove him to sourdough.

"Might bust down and have to sleep out," he meditated. "Then, agin, I ain't liable to; and if I do, I'll be goin' so fast I'll git somewhere before she stops. I'm — sure — goin' to go!"

He cranked the battered car, straddled in over the edge on the driver's side and set his feet against the pedals with the air of a man who had urgent business elsewhere. The men from Tonopah were not yet out of sight around the butte scarred with rhyolite ledges before Casey was under way, rattling down the rough trail from Starvation Mountain and bouncing clear of the seat as the car lurched over certain rough spots.

Pinned with a safety pin to the inside pocket of the vest he wore only when he felt need of a safe and secret pocket, Casey Ryan carried a check for twenty-five thousand dollars, made payable to himself. A check for twenty-five thousand dollars in Casey's pocket was like a wildcat clawing at his imagination and spitting at every moment's delay. Casey had endured solitude and some hardship while he coaxed Starvation Mountain to reveal a little of its secret treasure. Now he wanted action, light, life and plenty of it. While he drove he dreamed, and his dreams beckoned, urged him faster and faster.

Up over the summit of the ridge that lay between Starvation and Furnace Lake he surged, with radiator bubbling. Down the long slope to the lake, lying there smiling sardonically at a world it loved to trick with its moods, Casey drove as if he were winning a bet. Across that five miles of baked, yellow-white clay he raced, his Ford a-creak in every joint.

"Go it, you tin lizard!" chortled Casey. "I'll have me a real wagon when I git to Los. She'll be white, with red stripes along her sides and red wheels, and she'll lay 'er belly to the ground and eat up the road and lick her chops for more. Sixty miles under her belt every time the clock strikes, or she ain't good enough fer Casey! Mebby they think they got some drivers in Californy. Mebby they *think* they have. They ain't, though, because Casey Ryan ain't there yet. I'll catch that night train. Oughta be in by morning, and then you keep your eye on Casey. There's goin' to be a stir around Los, about to-morrow noon. I'll have to buy some clothes, I guess. And I'll git acquainted with some nice girl with yella hair that likes pleasure, and take

CASEY RYAN 41

her out ridin'. Yeah, I'll have to git me a swell outfit uh clothes. I'll look the part, all right —"

Up a long, winding trail and over another summit to Yucca Pass Casey dreamed, while the stark, scarred buttes on either side regarded him with enigmatic calm. Since the first wagon train had worried over the rough deserts on their way to California, the bleak hills of Nevada had listened while prospectors dreamed aloud and cackled over their dreaming; had listened, too, while they raved in thirst and heat and madness. Inscrutably they watched Casey as he hurried by with his twenty-five thousand dollars and his pleasant pictures of soft ease.

At a dim fork in the trail Casey slowed and stopped. A boiling radiator will not forever brook neglect, and Casey brought his mind down to practical things for a space. " I can just as well take the train from Lund," he mused, while he poured in more water. " Then I can leave this bleatin' burro with Bill. He oughta give me a coupla hundred for her, anyway. No use wasting money just because you happen to have a few thousand in your pants." He filled his pipe at that sensible idea and turned the nose of his Ford down the dim trail to Lund.

Eighty miles more or less straight away across the mountainous waste lay Lund, halfway up a canyon that led to higher reaches in the hills, rich in silver, lead, copper, gold. Silver it was that Casey had found and sold to the men from Tonopah, and it was a freak of luck, he thought whimsically, that had led him and his Ford away over to Starvation got to eat when the sun flirted with the scurrying clouds over his wind-torn automobile top.

So he came bouncing and swaying down the last mesa to the place called Red Lake. Casey had heard it spoken of with opprobrious epithets by men who had crossed it in wet weather. In dry weather it was red clay caked and checked by the sun, and wheels or hoofs stirred clouds of red dust that followed and choked the traveler.

Casey was not thinking at all of the lake when he drove down to it. He was seeing visions, though you would not think it to look at him; a stocky, middle-aged man who needed a shave and a hair-cut, wearing cheap, dirt-stained overalls and a blue shirt and square-toed shoes studded thickly on the soles with hobnails worn shiny; driving a desert-scarred Ford with most of the paint gone and a front fender cocked up and flapping crazily, and tires worn down to the fabric in places. But his eyes were very keen and steady, and there was a humorous twist to his mouth. If he dreamed incongruously of big, luxurious cars gorgeous in paint and nickel trim, and of slim young women with yellow hair and blue eyes,— well, stranger dreams have been hidden away behind exteriors more unsightly than was the shell which holds the soul of Casey Ryan.

Presently the practical, everyday side of his nature nudged him into taking note of his immediate surroundings. Red Lake had received a wetting. The dark, shiny surface betrayed that fact, and it was surprising how real water, when you did see it on a lake subject to mirage, was so unmistakably real. It is like putting flakes of real gold beside flakes of mica; you are ready to swear that the mica is gold,— until you see the real gold beside it. So Casey knew at a glance that half of Red Lake was wet, and that the shiny patches here and there were not mirage pictures but shallow pools of water. Moreover, out in the reddest, wettest part of it an automobile stood with its back to him, and pigmy figures were moving slowly upon either side.

the footlights, I could raise the price of admission and get away with it. How far is it to Rhyolite?"

"Rhyolite? Twenty or twenty-five miles, mebby." Casey gave him an inquiring look.

"Can we get there in time to paper the town and hire a hall to show in, Mister?" Casey saw the mud-caked feet move laboriously toward the rear of the car.

"Yes, ma'am, I guess you can. There ain't any town, though, and it ain't got any hall in it, nor anybody to go to a show."

The woman laughed. "That's like my prayer book. Well, Jack, you certainly have got a powerful eye, but you've been trying to Svengali this outfit out of the mud for an hour, and I haven't seen it move an inch, so far. Let's just try something else."

"A prayer outa your prayer book, maybe," her husband retorted, not troubling to move or turn his head.

Casey blinked and looked again. The woman who appeared from the farther side of the car might have been the creature of his dream, so far as her face, her hair and her voice went. Her hair was yellow, unmistakably yellow. Her eyes were bluer than Casey's own, and she had nice teeth and showed them in a red-lipped smile. A more sophisticated man would have known that the powder on her nose was freshly applied, and that her reason for remaining so long hidden from his sight while she talked to him was revealed in the moist color on her lips and the fresh bloom on her cheeks. Casey was not real. It is like putting flakes of real gold beside flakes of mica; you are ready to swear that the mica is gold,— until you see the real gold beside it. So Casey knew at a glance that half of Red Lake was wet, and that the shiny patches here and there were not mirage pictures but shallow pools of water. Moreover, out in the reddest, wettest part of it an automobile stood with its back to him, and pigmy figures were moving slowly upon either side.

CHAPTER VI

"Stuck," diagnosed Casey in one word, as he caught sight of the group ahead. He tucked his dream into the back of his mind while he pulled down the gas lever a couple of notches and lunged along the muddy ruts that led straight away from the safe line of sagebrush and out upon the platter-like red expanse.

The Ford grunted and lugged down to a steady pull, but Casey drove as he had driven his six horses on a steep grade in the old days, coaxing every ounce of power into action. He juggled with spark and gas and somehow kept her going, and finally stopped with nice judgment on a small island of harder clay within shouting distance of the car ahead. He killed the engine then and stepped down, and went picking his way carefully out to it, his heavy shoes speedily collecting great pancakes of mud that clung like glue.

"Stuck, hey? You oughta kept in the ruts, no matter if they are water-logged. You never want to turn outa the road on one of these lake beds, huntin' dry ground. If it's wet in the road, you can bank on sinkin' in to the hocks the minute you turn out." He carefully removed the mud pancakes from his shoes by scraping them across the hub of the stalled car and edged back to stand with his arms on his hips while he surveyed the full plight of them.

"She sure is bogged down a-plenty," he observed, grinning sympathetically.

"Could you hitch on your car, Mister, and pull us out?" This was a woman's voice, and it thrilled Casey, woman hungry as he was.

Casey put up a hand to his mouth and surreptitiously removed a chew of tobacco almost fresh. With some effort he pulled his feet closer together, and he lifted his old Stetson and reset it at a consciously rakish angle. He glanced at the car, behind it and in front, coming back to the depressed male individual before him. "Yes, ma'am, I'll get you out, all right. Sure, I will."

"We've been stalled here for an hour or more," volunteered the depressed one. "We was right behind the storm. Looked a sorry chance that anybody would come along for the next week or so."

"Mister, you're a godsend, if ever there was one. I'd write your name on the roster of saints in my prayer book, if I ever said prayers and had a prayer book and a pencil and knew what name to write."

"Casey Ryan. Don't you worry, ma'am. We'll get you outa here in no time." Casey grinned and craned his neck. Looking lower this time, he saw a pair of feet which did not seem to belong to that voice, though they were undoubtedly feminine. Still, red mud will work miracles of disfigurement, and Casey was an optimist by nature.

"My wife is trying out a new comedy line," the man observed unemotionally. "Trouble is it never gets over, out front. If she ever did get it across the footlights, I could raise the price of admission and get away with it. How far is it to Rhyolite?"

"Rhyolite? Twenty or twenty-five miles, mebby." Casey gave him an inquiring look.

"Can we get there in time to paper the town and hire a hall to show in, Mister?" Casey saw the mud-caked feet move laboriously toward the rear of the car.

"Yes, ma'am, I guess you can. There ain't any town, though, and it ain't got any hall in it, nor anybody to go to a show."

The woman laughed. "That's like my prayer book. Well, Jack, you certainly have got a powerful eye, but you've been trying to Svengali this outfit out of the mud for an hour, and I haven't seen it move an inch, so far. Let's just try something else."

"A prayer outa your prayer book, maybe," her husband retorted, not troubling to move or turn his head.

Casey blinked and looked again. The woman who appeared from the farther side of the car might have been the creature of his dream, so far as her face, her hair and her voice went. Her hair was yellow, unmistakably yellow. Her eyes were bluer than Casey's own, and she had nice teeth and showed them in a red-lipped smile. A more sophisticated man would have known that the powder on her nose was freshly applied, and that her reason for remaining so long hidden from his sight while she talked to him was revealed in the moist color on her lips and the fresh bloom on her cheeks. Casey was not

CASEY RYAN 49

sophisticated. He thought she was a beautiful woman and asked no questions of her make-up box.

"Mister, you certainly are a godsend!" she gushed again when she faced him. "I'd call you a direct answer to prayer, only I haven't been praying. I've been trying to tell Jack that the shovel is not packed under the banjos, as he thinks it was, but was left back at our last camp where he was trying to dig water out of a wet spot. Jack, dear, perhaps the gentleman has got a shovel in his car. Ain't it a real gag, Mister, us being stuck out here in a dry lake?"

Casey touched his hat and grinned and tried not to look at her too long. Husbands of beautiful young women are frequently jealous, and Casey knew his place and meant to keep it.

All the way back to his car Casey studied the peculiar features of the meeting. He had been thinking about yellow-haired women — well! But of course, she was married, and therefore not to be thought of save as a coincidence; still, Casey rather regretted the existence of Jack dear, and began to wonder why good-looking women always picked such dried-up little runts for husbands. "Show actors by the talk," he mused. "I wonder now if she don't sing, mebby?"

He started the car and forged out to them, making the last few rods in low gear and knowing how risky it was to stop. They were rather helpless, he had to admit, and did all the standing around while Casey did all the work. But he shoveled the rear wheels out, waded back to the tiny island of solid ground and gathered an armful of brush, which he crowded in front of the wheels, covering himself with mud thereby; then he tied the tow rope he carried for emergencies like this, waded to the Ford, cranked and trusted the rest to luck. The Ford moved slowly ahead until the rope between the two cars tightened, then spun her wheels and proceeded to dig herself in where she stood. The other car, shaking with the tremor of its own engine, ruthlessly ground the sagebrush into the mud and stood upon it roaring and spluttering furiously.

"Nothing like sticking together, Mister," called the lady cheerfully, and he heard her laughter above the churn of their motors.

"Say, ain't your carburetor all off?" Casey leaned out to call back to the husband. "You're smokin' back there like wet wood."

The man immediately stopped the motor and looked behind him.

Casey muttered something under his breath when he climbed out. He looked at his own car standing hub deep in red mud and reached for the solacing plug of chewing tobacco. Then he thought of the lady and withdrew his hand empty.

"We're certainly going to stick together, Mister," she repeated her witticism, and Casey grinned foolishly.

"She'll dry up in a few hours, with this hot sun," he observed hearteningly. "We'll have to pile brush in, I guess." His glance went back to the tiny island and to his double row of tracks. He looked at the man.

CASEY RYAN 51

"Jack, dear, you might go help the gentleman get some brush," the lady suggested sweetly.

"This ain't my act," Jack dear objected. "I just about broke my spine trying to heave the car outa the mud when we first stuck. Say, I wish there was a beanery of some kind in walking distance. Honest, I'll be dead of starvation in another hour. What's the chance of a bite, Hon?"

Contempt surged through Casey. Deep in his soul he pitied her for being tied to such an insect. Immediately he was glad that she had spirit enough to put the little runt in his place.

"You *would* wait to buy supplies in Rhyolite, remember," she reminded her husband calmly. "I guess you'll have to wait till you get there. I've got one piece of bread saved for Junior. You and I go hungry — and cheer up, old dear; you're used to it!"

"I've got grub," Casey volunteered hospitably. "Didn't stop to eat yet. I'll pack the stuff back there to dry ground and boil some coffee and fry some bacon." He looked at the woman and was rewarded by a smile so brilliant that Casey was dazzled.

"You certainly are a godsend," she called after him, as he turned away to his own car. "It just happens that we're out of everything. It's so hard to keep anything on hand when you're traveling in this country, with towns so far apart. You just run short before you know it."

Casey thought that the very scarcity of towns compelled one to avoid running short of food, but he did not say anything. He waded back to the island with a full load of provisions and cooking utensils, and in three minutes he was squinting against the smoke of a camp-fire while he poured water from a canteen into his blackened coffee pot.

"Coffee! Jack, dear, can you believe your nose!" chirped the woman presently behind Casey. "Junior, darling, just smell the bacon! Isn't he a nice gentleman? Go give him a kiss like a little man."

Casey didn't want any kiss — at least from Junior. Junior was six years old, and his face was dirty and his eyes were old, old eyes, but brown like his father's. He had the pinched, hungry look which Casey had seen only amongst starving Indians, and after he had kissed Casey perfunctorily he snatched the piece of raw bacon which Casey had just sliced off, and tore at it with his teeth like a hungry pup.

Casey affected not to notice, and busied himself with the fire while the woman reproved Junior half-heartedly in an undertone, and laughed stagily and remarked upon the number of hours since they had breakfasted.

Casey tried not to watch them eat, but in spite of himself he thought of a prospector whom he had rescued last summer after a five-day fast. These people ate more than the prospector had eaten, and their eyes followed greedily every mouthful which Casey took, as if they grudged him the food. Wherefore Casey did not take as many mouthfuls as he would have liked.

"This desert air certainly does put an edge on one's appetite," the woman smiled, while she blew across her fourth cup of coffee to cool it, and between breaths bit into a huge bacon sandwich, which Casey could not help knowing was her third. "Jack, dear, isn't this coffee delicious!"

"*Mah*-ma! Do we have to p-pay that there g-godsend? C-can you p-pay for more b-bacon for me, mah-ma?" Junior licked his fingers and twitched a fold of his mother's soiled skirt.

"Sure, give him more bacon! All he wants. I'll fry another skillet full," Casey spoke hurriedly, getting out the piece which he had packed away in the bag.

"He's used to these hold-up joints where they charge you forty cents for a greasy plate," the man explained, speaking with his mouth full. "Eat all yuh want, Junior. This is a barbecue and no collection took up to pay the speaker of the day."

"We certainly appreciate your kindness, Mister," the woman put in graciously, holding out her cup. "What we'd have done, stuck here in the mud with no provisions and no town within miles, heaven only knows. Was you kidding us," she added, with a betrayal of more real anxiety than she intended, "when you said Rhyolite is a dead one? We looked it up on the map, and it was marked like a town. We're making all the little towns that the road shows mostly miss. We give a fine show, Mister. It's been played on all the best time in the country — we took it abroad before the war and made real good money with it. But we just wanted to see the country, you know — after doing the cont'nent and all the like of that. So we thought we'd travel independent and make all the small towns —"

"The movie trust is what put vodeville on the bum," the man interrupted. "We used to play the best time only. We got a first-class act. One that ought to draw down good money anywhere, and would draw down good money, if the movie trust —"

"And then we like to be independent, and go where we like and get off the railroad for a spell. Freedom is the breath of life to he and I. We'd rather have it kinda rough now and then to be free and independent —"

"I've g-got a b-bunny, a-and it f-fell in the g-grease box a-and we c-can't wash it off, a-and h-he's asleep now. C-can I g-give my b-bunny some b-bacon, Mister G-godsend?"

The woman laughed, and Jack dear laughed, and Casey himself grinned sheepishly. Casey did not want to be called a godsend, and he hated the term "Mister" when applied to himself. All his life he had been plain Casey Ryan and proud of it, and his face was very red when he confessed that there was no more bacon. He had not expected to feed a family when he left camp that morning, but had taken rations for himself only.

Junior whined and insisted that he wanted b-bacon for his b-bunny, and the man hushed him querulously and asked Casey what the chances were for getting under way. Casey repacked a lightened bag, emptied the coffee grounds, shouldered his canteen

CASEY RYAN 55

and waded back to the cars and to the problem of red mud with an unbelievable quality of tenacity.

The man followed and asked him if he happened to have any smoking tobacco, afterwards he begged a cigarette paper, and then a match. "The doggone helpless, starved bunch!" Casey muttered, while he dug out the wheels of his Ford, and knew that his own haste must wait upon the need of these three human beings whom he had never seen until an hour ago, of whose very existence he had been in ignorance, and who would probably contribute nothing whatever to his own welfare or happiness, however much he might contribute to theirs.

I do not say that Casey soliloquised in this manner while he was sweating there in the mud under hot midday. He did think that now he would no doubt miss the night train to Los Angeles, and that he would not, after all, be purchasing glad raiment and a luxurious car on the morrow. He regretted that, but he did not see how he could help it. He was Casey Ryan, and his heart was soft to suffering even though a little of the spell cast by the woman's blue eyes and her golden hair had dimmed for him.

He still thought her a beautiful woman who was terribly mismated, but he felt vaguely that women with beautiful golden hair should not drink their coffee aloud, or calmly turn up the bottom of their skirts that they might use the underside of the hem for a napkin after eating bacon. I do not like to mention this; Casey did not like to think of it, either. It was with reluctance that he reflected upon the different standard imposed by sex. A man, for instance, might wipe his fingers on his pants and look the world straight in the eye,— but dog-gone it, when a lady's a lady, she ought to *be* a lady.

Later Casey forgot for a time the incident of the luncheon on Red Lake. With infinite labor and much patience he finally extricated himself and the show people, with no assistance from them save encouragement. He towed them to dry land, untied and put away his rope and then discovered that he had not the heart to drive on at his usual hurtling pace and leave them to follow. There was an ominous stutter in their motor, for one thing, and Casey knew of a stiffish hill a few miles this side of Rhyolite, so he forced himself to set a slow pace which they could easily follow.

CHAPTER VII

It was full sundown when they reached Rhyolite, which was not a town but a camp beside a spring, usually deserted. Three years before, a mine had built the camp for the accommodation of the truck drivers who hauled ore to Lund and were sometimes unable to make the trip in one day. Casey, having adapted his speed to that of the decrepit car of the show people, was thankful that they arrived at all. He still had a little flour and coffee and salt, and he hoped there was enough grease left on the bacon paper to grease the skillet so that bannocks would not stick to the pan. He also hoped that his flour would hold out under the onslaught of their appetites.

But Casey was lucky. A half dozen cowboys were camped there with a pack outfit, meaning to ride the canyons next day for cattle. They were cooking supper, and they had "beefed a critter" that had broken a leg that afternoon running among rocks. Casey shuffled his responsibility and watched, in complete content, while the show people gorged on broiled yearling steaks. (I dislike to use the word gorge where a lady's appetite is involved, but that is the word which Casey thought of first.)

Later, the show people very amiably consented to entertain their hosts. It was then that Casey was once more blinded by the brilliance of the lady and forgot certain little blemishes that had seemed to him quite pronounced. The cowboys obligingly built a bonfire before the tent, into which the couple retired to set their stage and tune their instruments. Casey lay back on a cowboy's rolled bed with his knees crossed, his hands clasped behind his thinning hair, and smoked and watched the first pale stars come out while he listened to the pleasant twang of banjos in the tuning.

It was great. The sale of his silver claim to the men from Tonopah, the check safely pinned in his pocket, the future which he had planned for himself swam hazily through his mind. He was fed to repletion, he was rich, he had been kind to those in need. He was a man to be envied, and he told himself so.

Then the tent flaps were lifted and a dazzling, golden-haired creature in a filmy white evening gown to which the firelight was kind stood there smiling, a banjo in her hands. Casey gave a grunt and sat up, blinking. She sang, looking at him frequently. At the encore, which was livened by a clog danced to hidden music, she surely blew a kiss in the direction of Casey, who gulped and looked around at the others self-consciously, and blushed hotly.

In truth, it was a very good show which the two gave there in the tent; much better than the easiest going optimist would expect. When it was over to the last twang of a banjo string, Casey took off his hat, emptied into it what silver he had in his pockets and set the hat in the fireglow. Without a word the cowboys followed his example, turning pockets inside out to prove they could give no more.

Casey spread his bed apart from the others that night, and lay for a long while smoking and looking up at the stars and dreaming again his dream; only now the golden-haired creature who leaned back upon the deep cushions of his speedy blue car was not a vague bloodless vision, but a real person with nice teeth and a red-lipped smile, who called him Mister in a tone he thought like music. Now his dream lady sang to him, talked to him,— I consider it rather pathetic that Casey's dream always halted just short of meal time, and that he never pictured her sitting across the table from him in some expensive café, although Casey was rather fond of café lights and music and service and food.

Next morning the glamor remained, although the lady was once more the unkempt woman of yesterday. The three seemed to look upon Casey still as a godsend. They had talked with some of the men and had decided to turn back to Vegas, which was a bigger town than Lund and therefore likely to produce better crowds. They even contemplated a three-night stand, which would make possible some very urgent repairs to their car. Casey demurred, although he could not deny the necessity for repairs. It was a longer trail to Vegas and a rougher trail. Moreover, he himself was on his way to Lund.

"You go to Lund," he urged, "and you can stay there four nights if you want to, and give shows. And I'll take yuh on up to Pinnacle in my car while yours is gettin' fixed, and you can give a show there. You'd draw a big crowd. I'd make it a point to tell folks you give a fine show. And I'll git yuh good rates at the garage where I do business. You don't want nothin' of Vegas. Lund's the place you want to hit fer."

"There's a lot to that," the foreman of the cowboys agreed. "If Casey's willin' to back you up, you better hit straight for Lund. Everybody there knows Casey Ryan. He drove stage from Pinnacle to Lund for two years and never killed anybody, though he did come close to it now and again. I've saw strong men that rode with Casey and said they never felt right afterwards. Casey, he's a dog-gone good driver, but he used to be kinda hard on passengers. He done more to promote heart failure in them two towns than all the altitude they can pile up. But nobody's going to hold that against a good show that comes there. I heard there ain't been a show stop off in Lund for over a year. You'll have to beat 'em away from the door, I bet." Wherefore the Barrymores — that was the name they called themselves, though I am inclined to doubt their legal right to it — the Barrymores altered their booking and went with Casey to Lund.

They were not fools, by the way. Their car was much more disreputable than you would believe a car could be and turn a wheel, and the Barrymores recognized the handicap of its appearance. They camped well out of sight of town, therefore, and let Casey drive in alone.

Casey found that the westbound train had already

CASEY RYAN 61

gone, which gave him a full twenty-four hours in Lund, even though he discounted his promise to see the Barrymores through. There was a train, to be sure, that passed through Lund in the middle of the night; but that was the De Luxe, standard and drawing-room sleepers, and disdained stopping to pick up plebeian local passengers.

So Casey must spend twenty-four hours in Lund, there to greet men who hailed him joyously at the top of their voices while they were yet afar off, and thumped him painfully upon the shoulders when they came within reach of him. You may not grasp the full significance of this, unless you have known old and popular stage drivers, soft of heart and hard of fist. Then remember that Casey had spent months on end alone in the wilderness, working like a lashed slave from sunrise to dark, trying to wrest a fortune from a certain mountain side. Remember how an enforced isolation, coupled with rough fare and hard work, will breed a craving for lights and laughter and the speech of friends. Remember that, and don't overlook the twenty-five thousand dollar check that Casey had pinned safe within his pocket.

Casey had unthinkingly tossed his last dime into his hat for the show people at Rhyolite. He had not even skinned the coyote, whose hide would have been worth ten or fifteen dollars, as hides go. In the stress of pulling out of the mud at Red Lake, he had forgot all about the dead animal in his tonneau until his nose reminded him next morning that it was there. Then he had hauled it out by the tail and thrown it away. He was broke, except that he had that check in his pocket.

Of course it was easy enough for Casey to get money. He went to the store that sold everything from mining tools to green perfume bottles tied with narrow pink ribbon. The man who owned that store also owned the bank next door, and a little place down the street which was called laconically The Club. One way or another, Dwyer managed to feel the money of every man who came into Lund and stopped there for a space. He was an honest man, too,— or as honest as is practicable for a man in business.

Dwyer was tickled to see Casey again. Casey was a good fellow, and he never needed his memory jogged when he owed a man. He paid before he was asked to pay, and that was enough to make any merchant love him. He watched Casey unpin his vest pocket and remove the check, and he was not too eager to inspect it.

"Good? Surest thing you know. Want it cashed, or applied to your old checking account? It's open yet, with a dollar and sixty-seven cents to your credit, I believe. I'll take care of it, though it's after banking hours."

Casey was foolish. "I'll take a couple of hundred, if it's handy, and a check book. I guess you can fix it so I can get what money I want in Los. I'm goin' to have one hell of a time when I git there. I've earned it."

Dwyer laughed while he inked a pen for Casey's endorsement. "Hop to it, Casey. Glad you made

CASEY RYAN 63

good. But you'd better let me put part of that in a savings account, so you can't check it out. You know, Casey — remember your weak point."

"Aw — that's all right! Don't you worry none about Casey Ryan! Casey'll take care of himself — he's had too many jolts to want another one. Say, gimme a pair of them socks before you go in the bank. I'll pay yuh," he grinned, "when yuh come back with some money. Ain't got a cent on me, Dwyer. Give it all away. Twelve dollars and something. Down to twenty-five thousand dollars and my Ford auty-*mo*-bile — and Bill's goin' to buy that off me as soon as he looks her over to see what's busted and what ain't."

Dwyer laughed again as he unlocked the door behind the overalls and jumpers and disappeared into his bank. Presently he returned with a receipted duplicate deposit slip for twenty-four thousand eight hundred dollars, a little, flat check book and two hundred dollars in worn bank notes. "You ought to be independent for the rest of your life, Casey. This is a fine start for any man," he said.

Casey paid for the socks and slid the change for a ten-dollar bill into his overalls pocket, put the check book and the bank notes away where he had carried the check, and walked out with his hat very much tilted over his right eye and his shoulders swaggering a little. You can't blame him for that, can you?

As he stepped from the store he met an old acquaintance from Pinnacle. There was only one thing to do in a case like that, and Casey did it quite naturally. They came out of The Club wiping their lips, and the swagger in Casey's shoulders was more pronounced.

Face to face Casey met the show lady, which was what he called her in his mind. She had her arms clasped around a large paper sack full of lumpy things, and her eyes had a strained, anxious look.

"Oh, Mister! I've been looking all over for you. They say we can't show in this town. The license for road shows is fifty dollars, to begin with, and I've been all over and can't find a single place where we could show, even if we could pay the license. Ain't that the last word in hard luck? Now what to do beats me, Mister. We've just got to have the old car tinkered up so it'll carry us on to the next place, wherever that is. Jack says he must have a new tire by some means or other, and he was counting on what we'd make here. And up at that other place you've mentioned the mumps have broke out and they wouldn't let us show for love or money. A man in the drug store told me, Mister. We certainly are in a hole now, for sure! If we could give a benefit for something or somebody. Those men back there said you're so popular in this town, I believe I've got an idea. Mister, couldn't you have bad luck, or be sick or something, so we could give a benefit for you? People certainly would turn out good for a man that's liked the way they say you are. I'd just love to put on a show for you. Couldn't we fix it up some way?"

Casey looked up and down the street and found it practically empty. Lund was dining at that hour.

And while Casey expected later the loud greetings and the handshakes and all, as a matter of fact he had thus far talked with Bill, the garage man, with Dwyer, the storekeeper and banker, and with the man from Pinnacle, who was already making ready to crank his car and go home. Lund, as a town, was yet unaware of Casey's presence.

Casey looked at the show lady, found her gazing at his face with eyes that said please in four languages, and hesitated.

"You could git up a benefit for the Methodist church, mebby," he temporized. "There's a church of some kind here — I guess it's a Methodist. They most generally are."

"We'd have to split with them if we did," the show lady objected practically. "Oh, we're stuck worse than when we was back there in the mud! We'd only have to pay five dollars for a six-months' theater license, which would let us give all the shows we wanted to. It's a new law that I guess you didn't know anything about," she added kindly. "You certainly wouldn't have insisted on us coming if you'd knew about the license."

"It's a year, almost, since I was here," Casey admitted; "I been out prospecting."

"Well, we can just work it fine! Can't we go somewhere and talk it over? I've got a swell idea, Mister, if you'll just listen to it a minute, and it'll certainly be a godsend to us to be able to give our show. We've got some crutches amongst our stage props, and some scar patches, Mister, that would certainly make you up fine as a cripple. Wouldn't they believe it, Mister, if it was told that you had been in an accident and got crippled for life?"

In spite of his embarrassment, Casey grinned. "Yeah, I guess they'd believe it, all right," he admitted. "They'd likely be tickled to death to see me goin' around on crutches." He cast a hasty thought back into his past, when he had driven a careening stage between Pinnacle and Lund, strewing the steep trail with wreckage not his own. "Yeah, it'd tickle 'em to death. Them that's rode with me," he concluded.

"Oh, you certainly are a godsend! Duck outa sight somewhere while I go tell Jack dear that we've found a way open for us to show, after all!" While Casey was pulling the sag out of his jaw so that he could protest, could offer her money, do anything save what she wanted, the show lady disappeared. Casey turned and went back into The Club, remained five minutes perhaps and then walked very circumspectly across the street to Bill's garage. It was there that the Barrymores found him when they came seeking with their dilapidated old car, their crutches, their grease paint and scar patches, to make a cripple of Casey whether he would or no.

Bill fell uproariously in with the plan, and Dwyer, stopping at the garage on his way home to dinner, thought it a great joke on Lund and promised to help the benefit along. Casey, with three drinks under his belt and his stomach otherwise empty, wanted to sing,

"Hey, ole Bill! Can-n yuh play the fiddle-o?
Yes, by —"

and stuck there because of the show lady. Casey wouldn't have recognized Trouble if it had walked up and banged him in the eye. He said sure, he'd be a cripple for the lady. He'd be anything once, and some things several times if they asked him in the right way. And then he gave himself into the hands of Jack dear.

CHAPTER VIII

Casey looked battered and sad when the show people were through with him. He had expected bandages wound picturesquely around his person, but the Barrymores were more artistic than that. Casey's right leg was drawn up at the knee so that he could not put his foot on the ground when he tried, and he did not know how the straps were fastened. His left shoulder was higher than his right shoulder, and his eyes were sunken in his head and a scar ran down along his temple to his left cheek bone. When he looked in the glass which Bill brought him, Casey actually felt ill. They told him that he must not wash his face, and that his week's growth of beard was a blessing from heaven. The show lady begged him, with dew on her lashes, to play the part faithfully, and they departed, very happy over their prospects.

Casey did not know whether he was happy or not. With Bill to encourage him and give him a lift over the gutters, he crossed the street to a restaurant and ordered largely of sirloin steak and French fried potatoes. After supper there was a long evening to spend quietly on crutches, and The Club was just next door. A man can always spend an evening very quickly at The Club — or he could in the wet days — if his money held out. Casey had money

CASEY RYAN

enough, and within an hour he didn't care whether he was crippled or not. There were five besides himself at that table, and they had unanimously agreed to remove the lid. Moreover, there was a crowd ten deep around that particular table. For the news had gone out that here was Casey Ryan back again, a hopeless cripple, playing poker like a drunken Rockefeller and losing as if he liked to lose.

At eight o'clock the next morning Bill came in to tell Casey that the show people had brought up their car to be fixed, and was the pay good? Casey replied without looking up from his hand, which held a pair of queens which interested him. He'd stand good, he said, and Bill gave a grunt and went off.

At noon Casey meant to eat something. But another man had come into the game with a roll of money and a boastful manner. Casey rubbed his cramped leg and hunched down in his chair again and called for a stack of blues. Casey, I may as well confess, had been calling for stacks of blues and reds and whites rather often since midnight.

At four in the afternoon Casey hobbled into the restaurant and ate another steak and drank three cups of black coffee. He meant to go across to the garage and have Bill hunt up the Barrymores and get them to unstrap him for awhile, but just as he was lifting his left crutch around the edge of the restaurant door, two women of Lund came up and began to pity him and ask him how it ever happened. Casey could not remember, just at the moment, what story he had already told of his accident.

He stuttered — a strange thing for an Irishman to do, by the way — and retreated into The Club, where they dared not follow.

"H'lo, Casey! Give yuh a chance to win back some of your losin's, if you're game to try it again," called a man from the far end of the room.

Casey swore and hobbled back to him, let himself stiffly down into a chair and dropped his crutches with a rattle of hard wood. Being a cripple was growing painful, besides being very inconvenient. The male half of Lund had practically suspended business that day to hover around him and exchange comments upon his looks. Casey had received a lot of sympathy that day, and only the fact that he had remained sequestered behind the curtained arch that cut across the rear of The Club saved him from receiving a lot more. But of course there were mitigations. Since walking was slow and awkward, Casey sat. And since he was not a man to sit and twiddle thumbs to pass the time, Casey played poker. That is how he explained it afterwards. He had not intended to play poker for twenty-four hours, but tie up a man's leg so he can't walk, and he's got to do *something*.

Wherefore Casey played,— and did not win back what he had lost earlier in the day. Daylight grew dim, and some one came over and lighted a hanging gasoline lamp that threw into tragic relief the painted hollows under Casey's eyes, which were beginning to look very bloodshot around the blue of them.

Once, while the bartender was bringing drinks —

you are not to infer that Casey was drunk; he was merely a bit hazy over details — Casey pulled out his dollar watch and looked at it. Eight-thirty — the show must be pretty well started, by now. He thought he might venture to hobble over to Bill's and have those dog-gone straps taken off before he was crippled for sure. But he did not want to do anything to embarrass the show lady. Besides, he had lost a great deal of money, and he wanted to win some of it back. He still had time to make that train, he remembered. It was reported an hour late, some one said.

So Casey rubbed his strapped leg, twisting his face at the cramp in his knee and letting his companions believe that his accident had given him a heritage of pain. He hitched his lifted shoulder into an easier position and picked up another unfortunate assortment of five cards.

At ten o'clock Bill, the garage man, came and whispered something to Casey, who growled an oath and reached almost unconsciously for his crutches before trying to get up; so soon is a habit born in a man.

"What they raisin' thunder about?" he asked apathetically, when Bill had helped him across the gutter and into the street. "Didn't the crowd turn out like they expected?" Casey's tone was dismal. You simply cannot be a cripple for twenty-four hours, and sit up playing unlucky poker all night and all day and well into another night, without losing some of your animation; not even if you are Casey Ryan. "Hell, I missed that train again," he added heavily, when he heard it whistle into the railroad yard.

"Too bad. You oughta be on it, Casey," Bill said ominously.

At the garage the Barrymores were waiting for him in their stage clothes and make-up. The show lady had wept seams down through her rouge, and the beads on her lashes had clotted unbecomingly.

"Mister, you certainly have wished a sorry deal on to us," she exclaimed, when Casey came hobbling through the doorway. "Fifteen years on the stage and *this* never happened to us before. We've took our bad luck with our good luck and lived honest and respectable and self-respecting, and here, at last, ill fortune has tied the can on to us. I know you meant well and all that, Mister, but we certainly have had a raw deal handed out to us in this town. We — certainly — have!"

"We got till noon to-morrow to be outa the county," croaked Jack dear, shifting his Adam's apple rapidly. "And that's real comedy, ain't it, when your damn county runs clean over to the Utah line, and we can't go back the way we come, or — and we can't go anywhere till this big slob here puts our car together. He's got pieces of it strung from here around the block. Say, what kinda town is this you wished on to us, anyway? Holding night court, mind you, so they could can us quicker!"

The show lady must have seen how dazed Casey looked. "Maybe you ain't heard the horrible deal they handed us, Mister. They stopped our show before we'd raised the curtain,—and it was a seventy-five dollar house if it was a cent!" she wailed. "They had a bill as long as my arm for license — we couldn't get by with the five-dollar one — and for lights and hall rent and what-all. There wasn't enough money in the house to pay it! And they was going to send us to jail! The sheriff acted anything but a gentleman, Mister, and if you ever lived in this town and liked it, I must say I question your taste!"

"We wouldn't use a town like this for a garbage dump, back home," cut in Jack with all the contempt he could master.

"And they hauled us over to their dirty old Justice of the Peace, and he told us he'd give us thirty days in jail if we was in the county to-morrow noon, and we don't know how far this county goes, either way!"

"Fifty miles to St. Simon," Bill told them comfortingly. "You can make it, all right —"

"We can make it, hey? How're we going to make it, with our car layin' around all over your garage?" Jack's tone was arrogant past belief.

Casey was fumbling for strap buckles which he could not reach. He was also groping through his colorful, stage-driver's vocabulary for words which might be pronounced in the presence of a lady, and finding mighty few that were of any use to him. The combined effort was turning him a fine purple when the lady was seized with another brilliant idea.

"Jack dear, don't be harsh. The gentleman meant well — and I'll tell you, Mister, what let's do! Let's trade cars till the man has our car repaired. Your car goes just fine, and we can load our stuff in and get away from this horrible town. Why, the preacher was there and made a speech and said the meanest things about you, because you was having a benefit and at the same identical time you was setting in a saloon gambling. He said it was an outrage on civilization, Mister, and an insult to the honest, hard-working people in Lund. Them was his very words."

"Well, hell!" Casey exploded abruptly. "I'm honest and hard-workin' as any damn preacher. You can ask anybody!"

"Well, that's what he said, anyhow. We certainly didn't know you was a gambler when we offered to give you a benefit. We certainly never dreamed you'd queer us like that. But you'll do us the favor to lend us your car, won't you? You wouldn't refuse that, and see me and little Junior languishin' in jail when you know in your heart —"

"Aw, take the darn car!" muttered Casey distractedly, and hobbled into the garage office where he knew Bill kept liniment.

Five minutes, perhaps, after that, Casey opened the office door wide enough to fling out an assortment of straps and two crutches.

The show lady turned and made a motion which Casey mentally called a pounce. "Oh, thank you, Mister! We certainly wouldn't want to go off and forget these props. Jack dear has to use them in a comedy sketch we put on sometimes when we got a good house."

Casey banged the door and said something exceedingly stage-driverish which a lady should by no means overhear.

Sounds from the rear of the garage indicated that Casey's Ford was r'arin' to go, as Casey frequently expressed it. Voices were jumbled in the tones of suggestions, commands, protest. Casey heard the show lady's clear treble berating Jack dear with thin politeness. Then the car came snorting forward, paused in the wide doorway, and the show lady's voice called out clearly, untroubled as the voice of a child after it has received that which it cried for.

"Well, good-by, Mister! You certainly are a godsend to give us the loan of your car!" There was a buzz and a splutter, and they were gone — gone clean out of Casey's life into the unknown whence they had come.

Bill opened the door gently and eased into the office, sniffing liniment. The painted hollows under Casey's eyes gave him a ghastly look in the lamplight when he lifted his face from examining a chafed and angry knee. Bill opened his mouth for speech, caught a certain look in Casey's eyes and did not say what he had intended to say. Instead:

"You better sleep here in the office, Casey. I've got another bed back of the machine shop. I'll lock up, and if any one comes and rings the night bell — well, never mind. I'll plug her so they can't ring her." The world needs more men like Bill.

Even after an avalanche, human nature cannot resist digging in the melancholy hope of turning up grewsome remains. I know that you are all itching to put shovel into the debris of Casey's dreams, and to see just what was left of them.

There was mighty little, let me tell you. I said in the beginning that twenty-five thousand dollars was like a wildcat in Casey's pocket. You can't give a man that much money all in a lump and suddenly, after he has been content with dollars enough to pay for the food he eats, without seeing him lose his sense of proportion. Twenty-five dollars he understands and can spend more prudently than you, perhaps. Twenty-five thousand he simply cannot gauge. It seems exhaustless. It is as if you plucked from the night all the stars you can see, knowing that the Milky Way is still there and unnumbered other stars invisible, even in the aggregate.

Casey played poker with an appreciative audience and the lid off. Now and then he took a drink stronger than root beer. He kept that up for a night and a day and well into another night. Very well, gather round and look at the remains, and if there's a moral, you are welcome, I am sure.

Casey awoke just before noon, and went out and held his head under Bill's garage hydrant, with the water running full stream. He looked up and found Bill standing there with his hands in his pockets, gazing at Casey sorrowfully. Casey grinned. You can't down the Irish for very long.

"How's she comin', Bill?"

Bill grunted and spat. "She ain't. Not if you mean that car them folks wished on to you. Well, the tail light's pretty fair, too. And in their hurry the lady went off and left a pink silk stockin' in the back seat. The toe's out of it though. Casey, if you wait till you overhaul 'em with that thing they wheeled in here under the name of a car —"

"Oh, that's all right, Bill," Casey grunted gamely. "I was goin' to git me a new car, anyway. Mine wasn't so much. They're welcome."

Bill grunted and spat again, but he did not say anything.

"I'll go see Dwyer and see how much I got left," Casey said presently, and his voice, whether you believe it or not, was cheerful. "I'm going to ketch that evenin' train to Los." And he added kindly, "C'm on and eat with me, Bill. I'm hungry."

Bill shook his head and gave another grunt, and Casey went off without him.

After awhile Casey returned. He was grinning, but the grin was, to a careful observer, a bit sickish. "Say, Bill, talk about poker — I'm off it fer life. Now look what it done to me, Bill! I puts twenty-five thousand dollars into the bank — minus two hundred I took in money — and I takes a check book, and I goes over to The Club and gits into a game. I wears the check book down to the stubs. I goes back and asks Dwyer how much I got in the bank, and he looks me over like I was a sick horse he had doubts about being worth doctorin', and as if he thought he mebby might better take me out an' shoot me an' put me outa my misery.

"'Jest one dollar an' sixty-seven cents, Casey,' he says to me, 'if the checks is all in, which I trust they air!'" Casey got out his plug of chewing tobacco and pried off a blunted corner. "An' hell, Bill! I had that much in the bank when I started," he finished plaintively.

"Hell!" repeated Bill in brief, eloquent sympathy.

Casey set his teeth together and extracted comfort from the tobacco. He expectorated ruminatively.

"Well, anyway, I got me some bran' new socks, an' they're paid for, thank God!" He tilted his old Stetson down over his right eye at his favorite, Caseyish angle, stuck his hands in his pockets and strolled out into the sunshine.

CHAPTER IX

"At that," said Bill, grinning a little, "you'll know as much as the average garage-man. What ain't reformed livery-stable men are second-hand blacksmiths, and a feller like you, that has drove stage for fifteen year—"

"Twenty," Casey Ryan corrected jealously. "Six years at Cripple Creek, and then four in Yellowstone, and I was up in Montana for over five years, driving stage from Dry Lake to Claggett and from there I come to Nevada—"

"Twenty," Bill conceded without waiting to hear more, "knows as much as a man that has kept livery stable. Then again you've had two Fords—"

"Oh, I ain't sayin' I can't *run* a garage," Casey interrupted. "I don't back down from runnin' anything. But if you'd grubstake me for a year, instead of settin' up this here garage at Patmos, I'd feel like I had a better chance of makin' us both a piece uh money. There's a lost gold mine I been wantin' fer years to get out and look for. I believe I know now about where to hit for. It ain't lost, exactly. There's an old Injun been in the habit of packin' in high grade in a lard bucket, and nobody's been able to trail him and git back to tell about it. He's an old she-bear to do anything with, but I got a scheme, Bill—"

"Ferget it," Bill advised. "Now you listen to me, Casey, and lay off that prospectin' bug for awhile. Here's this long strip of desert from Needles to Ludlow, and tourists trailin' through like ants on movin' day. And here's this garage that I can get at Patmos for about half what the buildin's worth. You ain't got any competition, none whatever. You've got a cinch. There'll be cars comin' in from both ways with their tongues hangin' out, outa gas, outa oil, needin' this and needin' that and looking on that garage as a godsend—"

"Say, Bill, if I gotta be a godsend I'll go out somewheres and holler myself to death. Casey's off that godsend stuff for life; you hear me, Bill—"

"Glad to hear it, Casey. If you go down there to Patmos to clean up some money for you 'n' me, you wanta cut out this soft-hearted stuff. Get the money, see? Never mind being kind; you can be kind when you've got a stake to be it with. Charge 'em for everything they git, and see to it that the money's good. Don't you take no checks. Don't trust nobody for anything whatever. That's your weakness, Casey, and you know it. You're too dog-gone trusting. You promise me you'll put a bell on your tire tester and a log chain and drag on your pump and jack — say, you wouldn't believe the number of honest men that go off for a vacation and steal everything, by golly, they can haul away! Pliers, wrenches, oil cans, tire testers — say, you sure wanta watch 'em when they ask yuh for a tester! You can lose more tire testers in the garage business —"

"Well, now, you watch Casey! When it comes to putting things like that over, they wanta try somebody besides Casey Ryan. You ask anybody if Casey's easy fooled. But I'd ruther go hunt the Injun Jim mine, Bill."

"Say, Casey, in this one summer you can make enough money in Patmos to *buy* a gold mine. I've been reading the papers pretty careful. Why, they say tourist travel is the heaviest that ever was known, and this is early May and it's only beginning. And lemme tell yuh something, Casey. I'd ruther have a garage in Patmos than a hotel in Los Angeles, and by all they say that's puttin' it strong. Ever been over the road west uh Needles, Casey?"

Casey never had, and Bill proceeded to describe it so that any tourist who ever blew out a tire there with the sun at a hundred and twenty and running in high, would have confessed the limitations of his own vocabulary.

"And there you are, high and dry, with fifteen miles of the ungodliest, tire-chewinest road on either side of yuh that America can show. About like this stretch down here between Rhyolite and Vegas. And hills and chucks — say, don't talk to me about any Injun packin' gold in a lard bucket. Why, lemme tell yuh, Casey, if you work it right and don't be so dog-gone kind-hearted, you'll want a five-ton truck to haul off your profits next fall. I'd go myself and let you run this place here, only I got a lot of credit trade and you'd never git a cent outa the bunch. And then you're wantin' to leave Lund for awhile, anyway."

"You could git somebody else," Casey suggested half-heartedly. "I kinda hate to be hobbled to a place like a garage, Bill. And if there's anything gits my goat, it's patchin' up old tires. I'll run 'em flat long as they'll stay on, before I'll git out and mend 'em. I'd about as soon go to jail, Bill, as patch tires for tourists; I —"

"You don't have to," said Bill, his grin widening. "You sell 'em new tires, see. There won't be one in a dozen you can't talk into a new tire or two. Whichever way they're goin', tell 'em the road's a heap worse from there on than what it was behind 'em. They'll buy new tires — you take it from me they will. And," he added virtuously, "you'll do 'em no harm whatever. If you got a car, you need tires, and a new one'll always come in handy sometime. You know that yourself, Casey.

"Now, I'll put in an assortment of tires, and I'll trust you to sell 'em. You and the road they got to travel. Why, when I was in Ludlow, a feller blew in there with a big brute of a car — 36-6 tires. He'd had a blow-out down the other side of Patmos and he was sore because they didn't have no tires he could use down there. He bought three tires — *three*, mind yuh, and peeled off the bills to pay for 'em! Sa-ay when yuh figure two hundred cars a day rollin' through, and half of 'em comin' to yuh with grief of some kind —"

"It's darn little I know about any car but a Ford," Casey admitted plaintively. "When yuh come to them complicated ones that you can crawl behind the wheel and set your boot on a button and

CASEY RYAN

holler giddap and she'll start off in a lope, I don't know about it. A Ford's like a mule or a burro. You take a monkey wrench and work 'em over, and cuss, and that's about all there is to it. But you take them others, and I got to admit I don't know."

"Well," said Bill, and spat reflectively, " you roll up your sleeves and I'll learn yuh. It'll take time for the stuff to be delivered, and you can learn a lot in two or three weeks, Casey, if you fergit that prospectin' idea and put your mind to it."

Casey rolled a cigarette and smoked half of it, his eyes clinging pensively to the barren hills behind Lund. He hunched his shoulders, looked at Bill and grinned reluctantly.

"She's a go with me, Bill, if you can't think of no other way to spend money. I wisht you took to poker more, or minin', or something that's got action. Stakin' Casey Ryan to a garage business looks kinda foolish to me. But if you can stand it, Bill, I can. It's kinda hard on the tourists, don't yuh think?"

Thus are garages born,— too many of them, as suffering drivers will testify. Casey Ryan, known wherever men of the open travel and spin their yarns, famous for his recklessly efficient driving of lurching stagecoaches in the old days, and for his soft heart and his happy-go-lucky ways; famous too as the man who invented ungodly predicaments from which he could extricate himself and be pleased if he kept his shirt on his back; Casey Ryan as the owner of a garage might justly be considered a joke pushed to the very limit of plausibility. Yet Casey

Ryan became just that after two weeks of cramming on mechanics and the compiling of a reference book which would have made a fortune for himself and Bill if they had thought to publish it.

"A quort of oil becomes lubrecant and is worth from five to fifteen cents more per quort when you put it into a two-thousand dollar car or over," was one valuable bit of information supplied by Bill. Also: "Never cuss or fight a man getting work done in your place. Shut up and charge him according to the way he acts."

It is safe to assume that Bill would make a fortune in the garage business anywhere, given normal traffic.

Patmos consists of a water tank on the railroad, a siding where trains can pass each other, a ten-by-ten depot, telegraph office and express and freight office, six sweltering families, one sunbaked lodging place with tent bedrooms so hot that even the soap melts, and the Casey Ryan garage. I forgot to mention three trees which stand beside the water tank and try to grow enough at night to make up for the blistering they get during the day. The highway (Coast to Coast and signed at every crossroads in red letters on white metal boards with red arrows pointing to the far skyline) shies away from the railroad at Patmos so that perspiring travelers look wistfully across two hundred yards or so of lava rock and sand and wish that they might lie under those three trees and cool off. They couldn't, you know. It is no cooler under the trees than elsewhere. It merely looks cooler.

Even the water tank is a disappointment to the uninitiated. You cannot drink the water which the pump draws wheezingly up from some deep reservoir of bad flavors. It is very clear water and it has a sparkle that lures the unwary, but it is common knowledge that no man ever drank two swallows of it if he could help himself. So the water supply of Patmos lies twelve miles away in the edge of the hills, where there is a very good spring. One of the six male residents of Patmos hauls water in barrels, at fifty cents a barrel. He makes a living at it, too.

One other male resident keeps the lodging place, — I avoid the term lodging house, because this place is not a house. It is a shack with a sign straddling out over the hot porch to insult the credulity of the passers-by. The sign says that this place is " The Oasis,"— and the nearest trees a long rifle-shot away, and the coolest water going warm into parched mouths!

The Oasis stands over by the highway, alongside Casey's garage, and the proprietor spends nine tenths of his waking hours sitting on the front porch and following the strip of shade from the west end to the east end, and in watching the trains go by, and counting the cars of tourists and remarking upon the State license plate.

"There's an outfit from Ioway, maw," he will call in to his wife. " Wonder where they're headed fer?" His wife will come to the door and look apathetically at the receding dust cloud, and go back somewhere,— perhaps to put fresh soap in the tents to melt. Toward evening the cars are very likely to slow down and stop reluctantly; sunburned, goggled women and men looking the place over without enthusiasm. It isn't much of a place, to be sure, but any place is better than none in the desert, unless you have your own bed and frying pan with you, roped in dusty canvas to the back of your car.

Alongside the Oasis stands the garage, and in the garage swelters Casey,— during this episode. Just at first Bill came down from Lund and helped him to arrange and mark prices on his stock of tires and " parts " and accessories, and to remember the catalogue names for things so that he would recognize them when a car owner asked for them.

Casey, I must explain, had evolved a system of his own while driving his Ford wickedly here and there to the consternation of his fellow men. Whatever was not a hootin'-annie was a dingbat, and treated accordingly. The hootin'-annie appeared to be the thing that went wrong, while the dingbat was the thing the hootin'-annie was attached to. It was perfectly simple, to Casey and his Ford, but Bill thought it was a trifle limited and was apt to confuse customers. So Bill remained three days mopping his face with his handkerchief and explaining things to Casey. After that Casey hired a heavy-eyed young Mexican to pump tires and fill radiators and the like, and settled down to make his fortune.

CHAPTER X

Cars came and cars went, in heat and dust and some tribulation. In a month Casey had seen the color of every State license plate in the Union, and some from Canada and Mexico. From Needles way they came, searching their souls for words to tell Casey what they thought of it as far as they had gone. And Casey would squint up at them from under the rim of his greasy old Stetson and grin his Irish grin.

"Cheer up, the worst is yet to come," he would chant, with never a qualm at the staleness of the slogan. "How yuh fixed for water? Better fill up your canteens — yuh don't wanta git caught out between here and Ludlow with a boilin' radiator and not water enough. Got oil enough? Juan, you look and see. Can't afford to run low on oil, stranger. No, ma'am, there ain't any other road — and if there was another road it'd be worse than what this one is. No, ma'am, you ain't liable to git off'n the road. You can't. You'd git stuck in the sand 'fore you'd went the length of your car."

He would walk around them and look at their tires, his hands on his hips perhaps and his mouth clamped shut in deep cogitation.

"What kinda shape is your extras in?" he would presently inquire. "She's a tough one, from here on to the next stop. You got a hind tire here that ain't goin' to last yuh five miles up the road." He would kick the tire whose character he was blackening. "Better lay in a supply of blow-out patches, unless you're a mind to invest in a new casing." Very often he would sell a tire or two, complete with new tubes, before the car moved on.

Casey never did things halfway, and Bill had impressed certain things deep on his mind. He was working with Bill's money and he obeyed Bill's commands. He never took a check or a promise for his pay, and he never once let his Irish temper get beyond his teeth or his blackened finger tips. Which is doing remarkably well for Casey Ryan, as you would admit if you knew him.

At the last moment, when the driver was settling himself behind the wheel, Casey would square his conscience for whatever strain the demands of business had put upon it. "Wait and take a good drink uh cold water before yuh start out," he would say, and disappear. He knew that the car would wait. The man or woman never lived who refused a drink of cold water on the desert in summer. Casey would return with a pale green glass water pitcher and a pale green glass. He would grin at their exclamations, and pour for them water that was actually cold and came from the coolest water bag inside. Those of you who have never traveled across the desert will not really understand the effect this would have. Those who have will know exactly what was said of Casey as that car moved out once more into the glaring sun and the hot wind and the choking dust.

Casey always kept one cold water bag and one in process of cooling, and he would charge as much as he thought they would pay and be called a fine fellow afterwards. He knew that. He had lived in dry, hot places before, and he was conscientiously trying to please the public and also make money for Bill, who had befriended him. You are not to jump to the conclusion, however, that Casey systematically robbed the public. He did not. He aided the public, helped the public across a rather bad stretch of country, and saw to it that the public paid for the assistance.

Casey saw all sorts and sizes of cars pass to and fro, and most of them stopped at his door, for gas or for water or oil, or perhaps merely to inquire inanely if they were on the right road to Needles or to Los Angeles, as the case might be. Any fool, thought Casey, would know without asking, since there was no other road, and since the one road was signed conscientiously every mile or two. But he always grinned good-naturedly and told them what they wanted him to tell them, and if they shifted money into his palm for any reason whatever he brought out his green glass pitcher and his green glass tumbler and gave them a drink all around and wished them luck.

There were strip-down Fords that tried to look like sixes, and there were six-cylinder cars that labored harder than Fords. There were limousines, sedans, sport cars,— and they all carried suitcases and canvas rolls and bundles draped over the hoods, on the fenders and piled high on the running boards.

Sometimes he would find it necessary to remove a thousand pounds or so of ill-wrapped bedding from the back of a tonneau before he could get at the gas tank to fill it, but Casey never grumbled. He merely retied the luggage with a packer's hitch that would take the greenhorn through his whole vocabulary before he untied it that night, and he would add two bits to the price of the gas because his time belonged to Bill, and Bill expected Casey's time to be paid for by the public.

One day when it was so hot that even Casey was limp and pale from the heat, and the proprietor of the Oasis had forsaken the strip of shade on his porch and had chased his dog out of the dirt hollow it had scratched under the house and had crawled under there himself, a party pulled slowly up to the garage and stopped. Casey was inside sitting on the ground and letting the most recently filled water bag drip down the back of his neck. He shouted to Juan, but Juan had gone somewhere to find himself a cool spot for his siesta, so Casey got slowly to his feet and went out to meet Trouble, sopping his wet hair against the back of his head with the flat of his hand before he put on his hat. He squinted into the sunshine and straightway squared himself for business.

This was a two-ton truck fitted for camping. A tall, lean man whose overalls hung wide from his suspenders and did not seem to touch his person anywhere, climbed out and stood looking at the bare rims of two wheels, as if he had at that moment discovered them.

CASEY RYAN 91

"Thinkin' about the price uh tires, stranger?" Casey grinned cheerfully. "It's lucky I got your size, at that. Fabrics and cords — and the difference in price is more'n made up in wear. Run yer car inside outa the sun whilst I change yer grief into joy."

"I been havin' hard luck all along," the man complained listlessly. "Geewhillikens, but it shore does cost to travel!"

Casey should have been warned by that. Bill would have smelled a purse lean as the man himself and would have shied a little. But Casey could meet Trouble every morning after breakfast and yet fail to recognize her until she had him by the collar.

"You ask anybody if it don't!" he agreed sympathetically, mentally going over his rack of tires, not quite sure that he had four in that size, but hoping that he had five and that he could persuade the man to invest. He surely needed rubber, thought Casey, as he scrutinized the two casings on the car. He stood aside while the man backed, turned a wide half-circle and drove into the grateful shade of the garage. It seemed cool in there after the blistering sunlight, unless one glanced at Casey's thermometer which declared a hundred and nineteen with its inexorable red line.

"Whatcha got there? Goats?" Casey's eyes had left the wheels of the trucks and dwelt upon a trailer penned round and filled with uneasy animals.

"Yeah. Twelve, not countin' the little fellers. And m'wife an' six young ones all told. Makes quite a drag on the ole boat. Knocks thunder outa tires, too. You say you got my size? We-ell, I guess I got to have 'em, cost er no cost."

"Sure you got to have 'em. It's worse ahead than what you been over, an' if I was you I'd shoe 'er all round before I hit that lava stretch up ahead here. You could keep them two fer extras in case of accident. Might git some wear outa them when yuh strike good roads again, but they shore won't go far in these rocks. You ask anybody."

"We-ell — I guess mebby I better — I don't see how I'm goin' to git along any other way, but —"

Casey had gone to find where Juan had cached himself and to pluck that apathetic youth from slumber and set him to work. Four casings and tubes for a two-ton truck run into money, as Casey was telling himself complacently. He had not yet sold any tires for a two-ton truck, and he had just two fabrics and two cords, in trade vernacular. He paid no further attention to the man, since there would be no bickering. When a man has only two badly chewed tires, and four wheels, argument is superfluous.

So Casey mildly kicked Juan awake and after the garage jack, and himself wheeled out his four great pneumatic tires, and with his jackknife slit the wound paper covering, and wondered what it was that smelled so unpleasant. A goat bleated plaintively to remind him of their presence. Another goat carried on the theme, and the chorus swelled quaveringly and held to certain minor notes. Within the closed truck a small child whimpered and then began to cry definitely at the top of its voice.

Casey looked up from bending over the fourth tire wrapping. "Better let your folks git out and rest awhile," he invited hospitably. "It's goin' to take a little time to put these tires on. I got some cold water back there — help yourself."

"Well, I'd kinda like to water them goats," the man observed diffidently. "They ain't had a drop sence early yest-day mornin'. You got water here, ain't yuh? An' they might graze around a mite whilst we're here. Travelin' like this, I try to kinda give 'em a chanct when we stop along the road. It's been an awful trip. We come clear from Wyoming. How far is it from here to San Jose, Californy?"

Casey had in the first week learned that it is not wise for a garage man to confess that he does not know distances. People always asked him how far it was to some place of which he had never heard, and he had learned to name figures at random very convincingly. He named now what seemed to him a sufficient number, and the man said "Gosh!" and went back to let down the end gate of the trailer and release the goats. "You said you got water for 'em?" he asked, his tone putting the question in the form of both statement and request.

When you are selling four thirty-six-sixes, two of them cords, to a man, you can't be stingy with a barrel of water, even if it does cost fifty cents. Casey told Juan to go borrow a tub next door and show the man where the water barrel stood. Juan, squatted on his heels while he languidly pumped the jack handle up and down, and seeming pleased than otherwise when the jack slipped and tilted so that he must lower it and begin all over again, got languidly to his bare feet and lounged off obediently. According to Juan's simple philosophy, to obey was better than to dodge hammers, pliers or monkey wrenches, since Casey's aim was direct and there was usually considerable force of hard, prospector's muscle behind it.

Juan was gone a long while, long enough to walk slowly to the station of Patmos and back again, but he returned with the tub, and the incessant bleating of the goats stilled intermittently while they drank. By this time Casey had forgotten the goats, even with the noise of them filling his ears.

Casey was down on his knees hammering dents out of the rim of a front wheel so that the new tire could go on. Four of the six offspring crowded around him, getting in the way of Casey's hammer and asking questions which no man could answer and remain normal. Casey had, while he unwrapped the casings, made a mental reduction in the price. Even Bill would throw off a little, he told himself, on a sale like this. Mentally he had deducted twenty-five dollars from the grand total, but before he had that rim straightened he said to himself that he'd be darned if he discounted more than twenty.

"Humbolt an' Greeley, you git away from there an' git out here an' git these goats a-grazin'," the lean customer called sharply from the rear of the garage. Humbolt and Greeley hastily proceeded to git, which left two unkempt young girls standing there at Casey's elbow so that he could not expectorate where he pleased, or swear at all. Wherefore Casey was appreciably handicapped in his work, and he wished that he were away out in the hills digging into the side of a gulch somewhere, sun-blistered, broke, more than half starving on short rations and with rheumatism in his right shoulder and a bunion giving him a limp in the left foot. He could still be happy —

"*What* yuh doin' that for?" the shrillest voice repeated three times rapidly, with a sniffle now and then by way of punctuation.

"To make little girls ask questions," grunted Casey, glancing around him for the snub-nosed, double-headed, four-pound hammer which he called affectionately by the name Maud. The biggest girl had Maud. She had turned it upright on its handle and was sitting on the head of it. When Casey reached for it and got it, without apology or warning, the girl sprawled backward and howled.

"Porshea, you git up from there! *Shame* on yuh!" A shrill woman voice, very much like the younger voices except that it was worn rough and querulous with age and many hardships, called down from the truck. Casey looked up, startled, and tried to remember just what he had said before the girls appeared to silence him. The woman was very large both in height and in bulk, and she was heaving herself out of the truck in a way that reminded Casey oddly of a disgruntled hippopotamus he had once watched coming out of its tank at a circus. Casey moved modestly away and did not look, after that first glance. A truck, you will please understand, is not a touring car, and ladies who have passed the two-hundred-pound notch on the scales should remain up there and call for a stepladder.

She descended, and the jack slipped and let the car down with a six-inch lurch. Casey is remarkably quick in his motions. He turned, jumped three feet and caught the lady's full weight in his arms as she was falling toward him. Probably he would have caught it anyway, but then there would have been little left of Casey, and his troubles would have been finished instead of being just begun.

He had just straightened the jack and was beginning to lift the bare wheel off the ground again when the fifth offspring descended. Casey thought again of the hippopotamus in its infancy. The fifth was perhaps fifteen, but she had apparently reached her full growth, which was very nearly that of her mother. She had also reached the age of self-consciousness, and she simpered at Casey when he assisted her to alight.

Casey was not bashful, nor was he over-fastidious; men who have lived long in the wilderness are not, as a rule. Still, he had his little whims, and he failed to react to the young lady's smile. His pale blue eyes were keen to observe details and even Casey did not approve of "high-water marks" on feminine beauty.

Well, that brought the whole family to view save the youngest who had evidently dropped asleep and was left in the truck. Casey went to work on the wheel again, after directing mother and daughter to the desert water bag which swung suspended from ropes in the rear of the garage.

Ten minutes later a dusty limousine stopped for gas and oil, and Casey left his work to wait upon them. There was a very good-looking girl driving, and the man beside her was undoubtedly only her father, and Casey was humanly anxious to be remembered pleasantly when they drove on. He asked them to wait and have a drink of cold water, and was deeply humiliated to find that both water bags were empty,— the overgrown girl having used the last to wash her face. Casey didn't like her any the better for that, or for having accentuated the high-water mark, or for forcing him to apologize to the pretty driver of the limousine.

He refilled the water bags and remarked pointedly that it would take an hour for the water to cool in them and that they must be left alone in the meantime. He did not look at the girl, but from the tail of his eye he saw her pull a contemptuous grimace at him when she thought his back safely turned.

Wherefore Casey finished the putting on of the fourth tire pretty well up toward the boiling point in temper and in blood. I have not mentioned half the disagreeable trifles that nagged at him during the interval,— his audience, for instance, that hovered so close that he could not get up without colliding with one of them, so full of aimless talk that he mislaid tools in his distraction. Juan was a pest and Casey thought malevolently how he would kill him when the job was finished. Juan went around like one in a trance, his heavy-lidded, opaque eyes following every movement of the girl, which kept her younger sisters giggling. But even with interruptions and practically no assistance the truck stood at last with four good tires on its wheels, and Casey wiped a perspiring face and let down the jack, thankful that the job was done; thinking, too, that ten dollars would be a big reduction on the price. He had to count his time, you see.

"Well, how much does it come to, mister?" the lord of the flock asked dolefully, when Casey called him in and told him that he could go at any time now.

Casey told him, and made the price only five dollars lower than the full amount, just because he hated to see men walk around loose in their pants, with their stomachs sagged in as though they never were fed a square meal in their lives.

"It's a pile uh money to pay out for rubber that's goin' to be chewed off on these here danged rocks," sighed the man.

Casey grunted and began collecting his tools, rescuing the best hammer he had from one of the girls. "I wisht it was all profit," he said. "Or even a quarter of it. I'm sellin' 'em close as I can an' git paid fer my time puttin' 'em on."

"Oh, I ain't kickin' about the price. I'm satisfied with that." Men usually are, you notice, when they want credit. "Now I tell yuh. I ain't got that much money with me —"

Casey spat and pointed his thumb toward a sign which he had nailed up just the day before, thinking that it would save both himself and his customers

CASEY RYAN

some embarrassment. The sign, except that the letters were not even, was like this:

"CHECKS MUST BE CASHED

BY THE ONER

OR THEY AIN'T CASHED"

The lean man read and looked at Casey humbly. "Well, I ain't never wrote a check in my life. Now I tell yuh. I ain't got the money to pay for these tires, but I tell yuh what I'll do; I'm goin' on up to my brother — he's got a prune orchard a little ways out from San Jose, an' he's well fixed. Now I'll write out an order on my brother, fer him to send you the money. He's good fer it, an' he'll do it. I'm goin' on up to help him work his place on shares, so I c'n straighten up with him when I get — "

Casey had picked up the jack again and was regretfully but firmly adjusting it under the front axle. "That ain't the first good prospect I ever had pinch out on me," he observed, trying to be cheerful over it. He could even grin while he squinted up at the lean man.

"Well, now, you can't hardly refuse to trust a man in my fix!"

"Think I can't?" Casey was working the jack handle rapidly and the words came in jerks. "You stand there and watch me." He spun the wheel free and reached for his socket wrench. "I wisht you'd spoke your piece before I set these darn nuts so tight," he added.

The lean man turned and looked inquiringly at his wife. "Ain't I honest, maw, and don't I pay my debts? An' ain't my brother Joe honest, an' don't he pay *his* debts? Would you think the man lived, maw, that would set a man with a fambly afoot out on the desert like this?"

"Nev' mind, now, paw. Give him time to think what it means, an' he won't. He's got a heart."

The baby awoke and cried then, and Casey's heart squirmed in his chest. But he thought of Bill and stiffened his business nerve.

"I got a heart; sure I've got a heart. You ask anybody if Casey's got a heart. But I also got a pardner."

"Your pardner's likely gen'l'man enough to trust us, if you ain't," maw said sharply.

"Yes, ma'am, he is. But he's got these tires to pay fer on the first of the month. It ain't a case uh not trustin'; it's a case of git the money or keep the tires. I wisht you had the money — she shore is a good bunch uh rubber I let yuh try on."

They wrangled with him while he removed the tires he had so painstakingly adjusted, but Casey was firm. He had to be. There is no heart in the rubber trust; merely a business office that employs very efficient bookkeepers, who are paid to see that others pay. He removed the new tires; that was his duty to Bill. By then it was five o'clock when all good mechanics throw down their pliers and begin to shed their coveralls.

Casey was his own man after five o'clock. He rolled the tattered tires out into the sunlight, let out the air and yanked them from their rims. "Come on here and help, and I'll patch up your old tires so you c'n go on," he offered good-naturedly, in spite of the things the woman had said to him. "The tire don't live that Casey can't patch if it comes to a showdown."

Before he was through with them he had donated four blow-out patches to the cause, and about five hours of hard labor. The Smith family — yes, they were of the tribe of Smith — were camped outside and quarreling incessantly. The goats, held in spasmodic restraint by Humbolt and Greeley and a little spotted dog which Casey had overlooked in his first inventory, were blatting inconsequently in the sage behind the garage. Casey cooked a belated supper and hoped that the outfit would get an early start, and that their tires would hold until they reached Ludlow, at least. "Though I ain't got nothin' against Ludlow," he added to himself while he poured his coffee.

"Maw wants to know if you got any coffee you kin lend," the shrill voice of Portia sounded unexpectedly at his elbow. Casey jumped,— an indication that his nerves had been unstrung.

"Lend? Hunh! Tell 'er I give her a cupful." Then, because Casey had streaks of wisdom, he closed the doors of the garage and locked them from the inside. Cars might come and honk as long as they liked; Casey was going to have his sleep.

Very early he was awakened by the bleating, the

barking, the crying and the wrangling of the Smiths. He pulled his tarp over his ears, hot as it was, to shut out the sound. After a long while he heard the stutter of the truck motor getting warmed up. There was a clamor of voices, a bleating of goats, the barking of the spotted dog, and the truck moved off.

"Thank Gawd!" muttered Casey, and went to sleep again.

CHAPTER XI

At two o'clock the next afternoon, the Smith outfit came back, limping along on three bare rims. Casey's jaw dropped a little when he saw them coming, but nature had made him an optimist. Now, perhaps, that hungry-looking Smith would dig into his pocket and find the price of new tires. It had been Casey's experience that a man who protested the loudest that he was broke would, if held rigidly to the no-credit rule, find the money to pay for what he must have. In his heart he believed that Smith had money dangling somewhere in close proximity to his lank person.

But if Smith had any money he did not betray the fact. He asked quite humbly for the loan of tools, and tube cement, and more blow-out patches, and set awkwardly to work mending his tattered tires. And once more Casey sent Juan to borrow the Oasis tub, and watered the goats and picked his way amongst the Smith offsprings and pretended to be deaf half of the time, and said he didn't know the other half. His green glass water pitcher was practically useless to travelers, and Juan was worse. A goat got away from Humbolt and Greeley and went exploring in the corner of the garage where

Casey lived, and ate three pounds of bacon. You know what bacon costs. Maw Smith became acquainted with Casey and followed him about with a detailed recital of her family history, which she thought would make a real exciting book. What Casey thought I must not tell you.

That night Casey patched tires and tubes. He had to, you see, or go crazy. Next morning he listened to the departure of the Smith family and the Smith goats, and prayed that their tires would hold out even as far as Bagdad,— though I don't see why, since there was no garage in Bagdad, or anything else but a flag station.

That afternoon at three o'clock, they came back again! And Casey neglected to send Juan after the tub to water the goats. Wherefore paw sent Humbolt, and watered the goats himself from Casey's barrel and seemed peevish because he must. Maw Smith came after coffee again, and helped herself with no more formality than a shrill, "I'm borrying some more coffee!" sent to Casey out in front.

That night Casey patched tires and tubes.

At six o'clock Smith pounded on the back door and called in to Casey that he would have to have some gas before he started. So Casey pulled on his pants and gave Smith some gas, and paid the garage out of his own pocket. He didn't swear, either. He was past that.

That afternoon Casey watched apprehensively the road that led west. It was two-thirty when he saw them coming. Casey set his jaw and went in and hid every blow-out patch he had in stock, and all the cement.

Smith went into camp, sent Greeley after the Oasis tub and watered the goats from one of Casey's water barrels. Casey went on with his work, waiting upon customers who paid, and tried not to think of the Smiths, although most of them were underfoot or at his elbow.

"Them tires you mended ain't worth a cuss," Smith came around finally to complain. "I didn't get ten mile out with 'em before I had another blowout. I tell yuh what I'll do. I'll trade yuh goats fer tires. I got two milk goats that's worth a hundred dollars apiece, mebby more, the way goats is selling on the Coast. I hate to part with 'em, but I gotta do somethin'. Er else you'll have to trust me till I c'n get to my brother an' git the money. It ain't," he added grievedly, "as if I wasn't honest enough to pay my debts."

"Nope," said Casey wearily, "I don't want yer goats. I've had more goats a'ready than I want. And tires has gotta roll outa this shop paid for. We talked that all over, the first night."

"What am I goin' to do, then?" Smith inquired in exasperation.

"Hell; I dunno," Casey returned grimly. "I quit guessin' day before yesterday."

Smith went off to confer with maw, and Casey overheard some very harsh statements made concerning himself. Maw Smith was so offended that she refused to borrow coffee from Casey that night, and she called her children out of his garage and told them she would warm their ears for them if they went near him again. Hearing which Casey's features relaxed a little. He could even meet customers with his accustomed grin when Smith in his anger sent the goats over to the water tank next day, refusing to show any friendship for Casey by emptying a water barrel for him. But he had to fire Juan for pouring gasoline into the radiator of a big sedan, and later he had to stalk that lovesick youth into the very camp of the Smiths and lead him back by the collar, and search him for stolen tools. He recovered twice as many as you would believe a Mexican's few garments could conceal.

Casey was harassed for two days by the loud proximity of the Smiths, but not one of them deigned to speak to him or to show any liking for him whatever, beyond helping themselves superciliously to the contents of his water barrel. On the morning of the third day the lean man presented his thin shadow and then himself at the front door of the garage, with a letter in his hand and a hopeful look on his face.

"Well, mebby I c'n talk business to yuh now an' have somethin' to go on," he began abruptly. "I went an' sent off a telegraft to my brother in San Jose about you, and he's wrote a letter to yuh. My brother's a business man. You c'n see that much fer yourself. An' mebby you'll see your way clear t' help me leave this dod-rotten hole. Here's yer letter."

Casey held himself neutral while he read the letter. As it happens that I have a copy, here it is:

(Printed Letterhead)
VISTA GRANDE RANCHO
Smith Bros.
San Jose, Calif.

Garage Owner, Patmos, Calif.

DEAR SIR: I am informed that my brother Eldreth William Smith, having suffered the mishap to lose his tires at your place or thereabouts, and having the misfortune to fall short of immediate funds with which to pay cash for replacement, has been denied credit at your hands.

I regret that because of business requirements in my own business it is impossible for me to place the amount necessary at his immediate disposal. It is therefore my advise that you lend to my brother Eldreth William Smith such money or moneys as will be necessary to purchase railroad tickets for himself and family from Patmos to this place, and

Furthermore that you take as security for said loan such motor truck and equipment etc. as he has now stored at your place of business. I am aware of the fact that a motor truck in any running condition would amply secure such loans as would purchase tickets from Patmos to San Jose, and I hereby enclose note for same, duly made out in blank and signed by me, which signature will be backed by the signature of my brother. Upon receiving from you such money as he may require he will duly deliver note and security duly signed and filled with the amount. I trust this will be perfectly satisfactory to you as amply securing you for the loan of the desired amount.

Thanking you in advance,

Yours very Truly,
J. PAUL SMITH.

In spite of himself, Casey was impressed. The very Spanish name of the prune orchard impressed him, and so did the formal business terms used by J. Paul Smith; and that " thanking you in advance " seemed to place him under a moral obligation too great to shirk. There was the note, too,— heavy green paper with a stag's head printed on it, and looking almost like a check.

" Well, all right, if it don't cost too much and the time don't run too long," surrendered Casey reluctantly. " How much —"

" Fare's a little over twenty-five dollars, an' they'll be four full fares an' three half. I guess mebby I better have a hundred an' seventy-five anyway, so'st we kin eat on the way."

Casey chanced to have almost that much coming to him out of the business, so that he would not be lending Bill's money. He watched the lean Smith fill in the amount and sign the note, identifying the truck by its engine and license numbers, and he went and borrowed fifteen dollars from the proprietor of the Oasis and made up the amount. There was a train at noon, and from his garage door he watched the Smith family start off across the lava rocks to the depot, each one laden with bundles and disreputable grips, the spotted dog trotting optimistically ahead of the party with his pink tongue draped over the right side of his mouth. Smith turned, the baby in his arms, and called back casually to Casey:

" Yuh better tie up them two milk goats when yuh milk 'em. They won't stand if yuh don't."

Casey's jaw sagged. He had not thought of the goats. Indeed, the last two days they had not troubled him except by their bleating at dawn. Humbolt and Greeley had grazed them over by the railroad track so that they could watch the trains go by. Casey looked and saw that the goats were still over there where they had been driven early. He took off his hat and rubbed his palm reflectively over the back of his head, set the hat on his head with a pronounced tilt over one eyebrow, and reached for his plug of tobacco.

"Oh, darn the goats! Me milkin' goats! Well, now, Casey Ryan never milked no goats, an' he ain't goin' to milk no goats! You can ask anybody if they think't he will."

Casey was very busy that day, and he had no dull-eyed Juan to do certain menial tasks about the cars that stopped before his garage. Nevertheless he kept an eye on the station of Patmos until the westbound train had come and had departed, and on the rough road between the railroad and the garage for another half hour, until he was sure that the Smith family were not coming back. Then he went more cheerfully about his work, now and then glancing, perhaps, at the truck which had been driven into the rear of the garage where it was very much in his way, but was safe from pilfering fingers. It was not such a bad truck, give it new tires. Casey had already figured the price at which he could probably sell it, on an easy payment plan, to the man who hauled water for Patmos. It was more than the amount of his loan, naturally. By noon he was rather hoping the " Smith Bros." would fail to take up that note.

Casey, you see, was not counting the goats at all. He had a vague idea that, while they were nominally a part of the security, they were actually of no importance whatever. They would run loose until Smith came after them, he guessed. He did not intend to milk any nanny goats, so that settled the goat question for Casey.

Casey simply did not know anything about goats. He ought to have used a little logic and not so much happy-go-lucky " t'ell with the goats." That is all very well, so far as it goes, and we all know that everybody says it and thinks it. But it does not settle the problem. It never occurred to Casey, for instance, that the going of Humbolt and Greeley and the little spotted dog would make any difference. It really did make a great deal, you see. And it never occurred to Casey that goats are domesticated animals after they have been hauled around the country for weeks and weeks in a trailer to a truck, or that they will come back to the only home they know.

I don't know how long it takes goats to fill up. I never kept a goat or goats. And I don't know how long they will stand around and blat before they start something. I don't know much more about goats than Casey, or didn't, at least, until he told me. By that time Casey knew a lot more, I suspect, than he could put into words.

Casey says that he heard them blatting around outside, but he was busy trying to straighten a radius rod — Casey *said* he was taking the kinks outa that hootin'-annie that goes behind the front ex and turns the dingbats when you steer — for a man who walked back and forth and slapped his hands together nervously and kept asking how long it was going to take, and how far it was to Barstow, and whether the road from there up across the Mojave was in good condition, and whether the Death Valley road out from Ludlow went clear through the valley and was a cut-off north, or whether it just went into the valley and stopped. Casey says that the only time he ever was in Death Valley it was with a couple of burros and that he like to have stayed there. He got to telling the man about his trip into Death Valley and how he just did get out by a scratch.

So he didn't pay any attention to the goats until he went back after some cold water for the white little woman in the car, that looked all tuckered out and scared. It was then he found the whole corner chewed off one water bag and the other water bag on the ground and a lot more than the corner gone. And the billy was up on his hind feet with his horns caught in the fullest barrel, and was snorting and snuffling in a drowning condition and tilting the barrel perilously. The other goats were acting just like plain damn goats, said Casey, and merely looking for trouble without having found any.

Casey says he had to call the Oasis man to help him get Billy out of the barrel, and that even then he had to borrow a saw and saw off one horn — either that, or cave in the barrel with Maud — and he needed that barrel worse than the billy goat needed two horns; but he told me that if he'd had Maud in his two hands just then he sure would have caved in the goat.

At that, the nervous man got away without paying Casey, which I think rankled worse than a spoiled barrel of water.

Casey told me that he aged ten years in the next two weeks, and lost eighty-nine dollars and a half in damages and wages, not counting the two water bags he had to replace out of his stock, at nearly four dollars wholesale price. When he chased the goats out of his back door they went around and came in at the front, determined, he supposed, to bed down near the truck.

It was late before that occurred to him, and when it did he cranked up and drove the truck a hundred yards down the road that led to the spring. The goats did not follow as he expected, but stood around the trailer and blatted. Casey went back and hooked on the trailer and drove again down the road. The goats would not follow, and he went back to find that Billy had managed to push open the back door and had led his flock into Casey's kitchen. There was no kitchen left but the little camp stove, and that was bent so that it stood skew-gee, Casey said, and developed a habit of toppling over just when his coffee came to a boil.

Casey told me that he had to barricade himself in his garage that night, and he swore that Billy stood on his hind feet and stared at him all night through the window in spite of wrenches and pliers hailing out upon him. However that may be, Billy couldn't have stood there all night, unless Casey got his dates mixed. For at six o'clock the Oasis man came over, stepping high and swinging his fists, and told Casey that them damn goats had et all the bedding out of one tent and the soap, towel and one pillow out of another, and what was Casey going to do about it?

Casey did not know,— and he was famous for his resourcefulness too. I think he paid for the bedding before the thing was settled.

Casey says that after that it was just one thing after another. He told me that he never would have believed twelve goats could cover so much cussedness in a day. He said he couldn't fill a radiator but some goat would be chewing the baggage tied behind the car, or Billy would be rooting suitcases off the running board. One party fell in love with a baby goat and Casey in a moment of desperation told them they could have it. But he was sorry afterward, because the mother stood and blatted at him reproachfully for four days and nights without stopping.

Casey swears that he picked up and threw two tons of rocks every day, and he has no idea how many tons the six families of Patmos heaved at and after the goats. When they weren't going headfirst into barrels of water they were chewing something not meant to be chewed. Casey asserts that it is all a bluff about goats eating tin cans. They don't. He says they never touched a can all the while he had them. He says devastated Patmos wished they would, and leave the two-dollar lace curtains alone, and clotheslines and water barrels and baggage. He says many a party drove off with chewed bedding rolls and didn't know it, and that he didn't tell them, either.

You're thinking about Juan, I know. Well, Casey thought of Juan the first day, and took the trouble to hunt him up and hire him to herd the goats. But Juan developed a bad case of sleeping sickness, Casey says, which unfortunately was not contagious to goats. He swears that he never saw one of those goats lying down, though he had seen pictures of goats lying down and had a vague idea that they chewed their cuds. Casey tried to be funny, then. He looked at me and grinned, and observed, "Hunh! Goats don't chew cuds. That's all wrong. They chew *duds*. You ask anybody in Patmos." So Juan slept under sagebushes and grease-wood, and the goats did not.

Casey declares that he stood it for two weeks, and that it took all he could make in the garage to pay the six families of Patmos for the damage wrought by his security. He lost fifteen pounds of flesh and every friend he had made in the place except the man who hauled water, and he liked it because he was getting rich. Once Casey had a bright idea, and with much labor and language he loaded the goats into the trailer and had the water-hauler take them out to the hills. But that didn't work at all. Part of the flock came back afoot, from sheer homesickness, and the rest were hauled back because they were ruining the spring which was Patmos' sole water supply.

Casey would have shot the goats, but he couldn't bring himself to do anything that would offend J. Paul Smith of the *Vista Grande Rancho*. Whenever he read the letter J. Paul Smith had written him he was ashamed to do anything that would lower him in the estimation of J. Paul Smith, who trusted him and took it for granted that he would do the right thing and do it with enthusiasm.

"If he hadn't wrote so dog-gone polite!" Casey complained to me. "And if he hadn't went an' took it for granted I'd come through. But a man can't turn down a feller that wrote the way he done. Look at that letter! A college perfessor couldn't uh throwed together no better letter than that. And that there 'Thanking you in advance'— a feller *can't* throw a man down when he writes that way. You ask anybody." Casey's tone was one of reminiscent injury, as if J. Paul Smith had indeed taken a mean advantage of him.

One day Casey reached the limit of his endurance,— or perhaps of the endurance of Patmos. There were not enough male residents to form a mob strong enough to lynch Casey, but there was one woman who had lost a sofa pillow and two lace curtains; Casey did not say much about her, but I gathered that he would as soon be lynched as remonstrated with again by that woman. "Sufferin' Sunday! I'd shore hate to be her husband. You ask anybody!" sighed Casey when he was telling me.

Casey moralized a little. "Folks used to look at the goats that I'd maybe just hazed off into the brush fifty yards or so with a thousand pounds mebby of rocks, an' some woman in goggles would say, 'Oh, an' you keep goats! How nice!' like as if it were something peaceful an' homelike to keep goats! Hunh! Lemme tell yuh; never drive past a place that *looks* peaceful, and jump at the idea it *is* peaceful. They may be a woman behind them vines poisinin' 'er husband's father. How could them darn tourists tell what was goin' on in Patmos? They seen the goats pertendin' to graze, an' keepin' an eye peeled till my back was turned, an' they thought it was *nice* to keep goats. Hunh!"

At last Casey could bear no more. He gathered together enough hardwood, three-inch crate slats to make twelve crates, and he worked for three nights, making them. And Casey is no carpenter. After that he worked for three days, with all the men in Patmos to help him, getting the goats into the crates and loaded on the truck. Then he drove over to the station and asked for tags, and addressed the crates to J. Paul Smith, *Vista Grande Rancho,* San Jose, Calif. Then he discovered that he could not send them except by express, and that he could not send them by express unless he prepaid the charges. And the charges on goats sent by express, was, as Casey put it, a holy fright.

But he had to do it. Patmos had been led to believe that he would send those goats off on the train, and Casey did not know what would happen if he failed. There were the heads of the six families, and all the children who were of walking age, grouped around the crates and Casey expectantly.

Casey went back to the garage safe and got what money he had, borrowed the balance from the male citizens of Patmos and prepaid the express. Patmos helped to load them into the first express car going west, and Casey felt, he said, as if some one had handed him a million dollars in dimes.

Casey seemed to think that ended the story, but I am like the rest of you. I wanted to know what the Smith family did, and J. Paul Smith, and whether Casey kept the truck and sold it to the man who hauled water.

"Who? Me? Say! D'you ever know Casey Ryan to ever come out anywheres but at the little end uh the horn? Ain't I the bag holder pro tem?" I don't know what he meant by that. I think he was mistaken in the meaning of "pro tem."

"You ask anybody. Say, I got a letter sayin' in a gen'ral way that I'm a thief an' a cutthroat an' a profiteer an' so on, an' that I would have to pay fer the goat that was missin'—that there was the one I give away — an' that the damages to the billy goat was worth twenty-five dollars and same would be deducted from the amount of the loan. *Darn* these fancy word slingers!" said Casey. "An' the day before the note come due, here comes that shoestring in pants with the money to pay the note minus the damages, and four new tires fer the truck! Yessir, wouldn't buy tires off me, even! Could yuh beat that fer gall? And he wouldn't hardly speak."

Casey grinned and got his plug of tobacco and inspected the corners absently before he bit into it. "But I got even with 'im," he added. "I laid off till he got his tires on — an' I wouldn't lend him no tools to put 'em on with, neither. And then I looked up an' down the road an' seen there was no dust comin' an' we wouldn't be interrupted, an' I went up to the old skunk an' I says, ' I got a bill to colleck off you. *Thankin' you in advance!*' an' then I shore collected. You ask anybody in Patmos. Say, I bet he drove by-guess-an'-by-gosh to the orange belt, anyway, the way his eyes was swellin' up when he left!"

I mentioned his promise to Bill, that he would not fight a customer. Casey spat disgustedly. " Hell! He wasn't no customer! Didn't he ship his rubber in by express, ruther'n to buy off me?" He grinned retrospectively and looked at his knuckles, one of which showed a patch of new skin, pink and yet tender.

"' Thankin' you in advance!' that's just what I told 'im. An' I shore got all I thanked 'im for! You ask anybody in Patmos. They seen 'im afterwards."

CHAPTER XII

"Look there!" Casey rose from the ground where he had been sitting with his hands clasped round his drawn-up knees. He pointed with his pipe to a mountain side twelve miles away but looking five, even in the gloom of early dusk. "Look at that, will yuh! Whadda yuh say that is, just makin' a guess? A fire, mebby?"

"Camp fire. Some prospector boiling coffee in a dirty lard bucket, maybe."

Casey snorted. "It's a darn big fire to boil a pot uh coffee! Recollect, it's twelve miles over to that mountain. A bonfire a mile off wouldn't look any bigger than that. Would it now?" His tone was a challenge to my truthfulness.

"Wel-l, I guess it wouldn't, come to think of it."

"Guess? You know darn well it wouldn't. You watch that there fire. I ain't over there — but if that ain't the devil's lantern, I'll walk on my hands from here over there an' find out for yuh."

"I'd have to go over there myself to discover whether you're right or wrong. But if a fellow can trust his eyes, Casey —"

"Well, you can't," Casey said grimly, still standing, his eyes fixed upon the distant light. "Not here in this country, you can't. You ask anybody. You don't trust your eyes when yuh come to a dry lake an' you see water, an' the bushes around the shore reflected in the water, an' mebby a boat out in the middle. *Do* yuh? You don't trust your eyes when you look at them hills. They look close enough to walk over to 'em in half or three quarters of an hour. *Don't* they? An' didn't I take yuh in my Ford auty-*mo*-bile, an' wasn't it twelve? An' d'yuh trust your eyes when yuh look up, an' it looks like you could knock stars down with a tent pole, like yuh knock apples off'n trees? Sure, you can't trust your eyes! When yuh hit the desert, ole-timer, yuh pack two of the biggest liars on earth right under your eyebrows." He chuckled at that. " An' most folks pack another one under their noses, fer luck. Now lookit over there! Prospector nothin'. It's the devil out walkin' an' packin' a lantern. He's mebby found some shin bones an' a rib or two an' mebby a chewed boot, an' he stopped there to have his little laugh. Lemme tell yuh. You mark where that fire is. An' t'-morra, if yuh like, I'll take yuh over there. If you c'n find a track er embers on that slope — Gawsh!"

We both stood staring; while he talked, the light had blinked out like snapping an electric switch. And that was strange because camp fires take a little time in the dying. I stepped inside the tent, fumbled for the field glasses and came out, adjusting the night focus. Casey's squat, powerful form stood perfectly still where I had left him, his face turned toward the mountain. There was no fire on the slope. Beyond, hanging black in the sky, a thunder cloud pillowed up toward the peak of the mountain, pushing out now and then to blot a star from the purple. Now and then a white, ragged gash cut through, but no sound reached up to where we were camped on the high mesa that was the lap of Starvation Mountain. I will explain that Casey had come back to Starvation to see if there were not another good silver claim lying loose and needing a location monument. We faced Tippipah Range twelve miles away,— and to-night the fire on its slope.

"Lightning struck a yucca over there and burned it, probably," I hazarded, seeking the spot through the glasses.

"Yeah — only there ain't no yuccas on that slope. That's a limestone ledge formation an' there ain't enough soil to cover up a t'rantler. And the storm's over back of the Tippipahs anyhow. It ain't on 'em."

"It's burning up again —"

"Hit another yucca, mebby!"

"It looks —" I adjusted the lenses carefully "— like a fire, all right. There's a reddish cast. I can't see any flames, exactly, but —" I suppose I gave a gasp, for Casey laughed outright.

"No, I guess yuh can't. Flames don't travel like that — huh?"

The light had moved suddenly, so that it seemed to jump clean away from the field of vision embraced by the glasses. I had a little trouble in picking it up again. I had to take down the glasses and look; and then I left them down and watched the light with my naked, lying eyes. They did lie; they must have. They said that a camp fire had abruptly picked itself up bodily and was slipping rapidly as a speeding automobile up a bare white slide of rock so steep that a mountain goat would give one glance and hunt up an easier trail. All my life I have had intimate acquaintance with camp fires; I have eaten with them, slept with them, coaxed them in storm, watched them from afar. I thought I knew all their tricks, all their treacheries. I have seen apparently cold ashes blow red quite unexpectedly and fire grass and bushes and go racing away,— I have fought them then with whatever came to hand.

I admit that an odd, prickly sensation at the base of my scalp annoyed me while I watched this fire race up the slope and leave no red trail behind it. Then it disappeared, blinked out again. I opened my mouth to call Casey's attention to it — though I felt that he was watching it with that steady, squinting stare of his that never seems to wink or waver for a second — but there it was again, come to a stop just under the crest of the mountain where the white slide was topped by a black rim capped with bleak, bare rock like a crude skullcap on Tippipah. The fire flared, dimmed, burned bright again, as though some one had piled on dry brush. I caught up the glasses and watched the light for a full minute. They were good glasses,—I ought to have seen the flicker of flames; but I did not. Just the reddish yellow glow and no more.

"Must be fox fire," I said, feeling impatient because that did not satisfy me at all, but having no other explanation that I could think of handy. "I've seen wonderful exhibitions of it in low, swampy ground —

Casey spat into the dark. "I never heard of nobody boggin' down, up there on Tippipah." He put his cold pipe in his mouth, removed it and gestured with it toward the light. "I've seen jack-o'-lanterns myself. You know darn well that ain't it; not up on them rocks, dry as a bone. A minute ago you said it was lightnin' burnin' a yucca. Why don't yuh come out in the open, an' say you don't *know*? Mebby you'll come closer to believin' what I told yuh about that devil's lantern I follered. He's lit another one — kinda hopin' we'll be fool enough to fall for it. You come inside where yuh can't watch it. That's what does the damage — watchin' and wonderin' and then goin' to see. I bet you wanta strike out right now and see just what it is."

I didn't admit it, but Casey had guessed exactly what was in my mind. I was itching with curiosity and trying to ignore the creepiness of it. Casey went into the tent and lighted the candle and proceeded to unlace his high hiking boots. "You come on in and go to bed. Don't yuh pay no attention to that light — that's what the Old Boy plays for first, every time; workin' your curiosity up. You ask anybody. He played me fer a sucker and I told yuh about it, and yuh thought Casey was stringin' yuh. Well, I can take a joke from the devil himself and never let out a yip — but once is enough for Casey! I'm goin' to bed. Let him set out there and hold his darn lantern and be damned; he ain't going to make nothin' off'n Casey Ryan this time.

You can ask anybody if Casey Ryan bites twice on the same hook."

He got into bed and turned his face to the wall with a finality I could not ignore. I let it go at that, but twice I got up and went outside to look. There burned the light, diabolically like a signal fire on the peak, where no fire should be. I began to seek explanations, but the best of them were vague. Electricity playing a prank of some obscure kind,— that was as close as I could get to it, and even that did not satisfy as it should have done, perhaps because the high, barren mesas and the mountains of bare rocks are in themselves weird and sinister, and commonplace explanations of their phenomena seem out of place.

The land is empty of men, emptier still of habitations. There are not many animals, even. A few coyotes, all of them under suspicion of having rabies; venomous things such as tarantulas and centipedes, scorpions, rattlers, hydrophobia skunks. Not so many of them that they are a constant menace, but occasionally to be reckoned with. Great sprawling dry lakes ominous in their very placidity; dust dry, with little whirlwinds scurrying over them and mirages that lie to you most convincingly, painting water where there is only clay dust. Water that is hidden deep in forbidding canyons, water that you must hunt for blindly unless you have been told where it comes stealthily out from some crevice in the rocks. Indians know the water holes, and have told the white men with whom they made friends after a fashion — for Casey tells me he never knew a red man who was essentially noble — and these have told others; and men have named the springs and have indicated their location on maps. Otherwise the land is dry, parched and deadly and beautiful, and men have died terrible, picturesque deaths within its borders.

I was thinking of that, and it seemed not too incongruous that the devil should now and then walk abroad with a lantern of his own devising to make men shrink from his path. But Casey says, and I think he means it, that the light is a lure. He told me a weird adventure of his own to back his argument, but I thought he was inventing most of it as he went along. Until I saw that light on Tippipah I had determined to let his romancing go in at one ear if it must, and stop there without running out at the tips of my fingers. Casey has enough ungodly adventures that are true. I didn't feel called upon to repeat his Irish inventions.

But now I'm going to tell you. If you can't believe it I shall not blame you; but Casey swears that it is all true. It's worth beginning where Casey did, at the beginning. And that goes back to when he was driving stage in the Yellowstone.

Casey was making the trip out, one time, and he had just one passenger because it was at the end of the season and there had been a week of nasty weather that had driven out most of the sightseers and no new ones were coming in. This man was a peevish, egotistical sort, I imagine; at any rate he did a lot of talking about himself and his ill luck, and he told Casey of his misfortunes by the hour.

Casey did not mind that much. He says he didn't listen half the time. But finally the fellow began talking of the wealth that is wasted on folks who can't use it properly or even appreciate the good fortune.

To illustrate that point he told a story that set Casey's mind to seeing visions. The man told about an old Indian who lived in dirt and a government blanket and drank bad whisky when he could get it, and whipped his squaw and behaved exactly like other Indians. Yet that old Indian knew where gold lay so thick that he could pick out pieces of crumbly rock all plastered with free gold. He was too lazy to dig out enough to do him any good. He would come into the nearest town with a rusty old lard bucket full of high grade so rich that the storekeeper once got five hundred dollars from the bucketful. He gave the Indian about twenty dollars' worth of grub and made him a present of two yards of bright blue ribbon, which tickled the old buck so much that in two weeks he was back with more high grade knotted in the bottom of a gunny sack.

Casey asked the man why some one didn't trail the Injun. Casey knew that an Indian is not permitted to file a claim to mineral land. He could not hold it, under the law, if some white man discovered it and located the ground, but Casey thought that some white-hearted fellow might take the claim and pay the buck a certain percentage of the profits.

The man said that couldn't be done. The old buck — Injun Jim, they called him — was an old she-bear. All the Indians were afraid of him and would hide their faces in their blankets when he passed them on his way to the gold, rather than be suspected by Injun Jim of any unwarranted interest in his destination. Casey knew enough about Indians to accept that statement. And white men, it would seem, were either not nervy enough or else they were not cunning enough. A few had attempted to trail Injun Jim, but no one had ever succeeded, because that part of Nevada had not had any gold stampede, which the man declared would have come sure as fate if Injun Jim's mine were ever uncovered.

Casey asked certain questions and learned all that the man could tell him,— or would tell him. He said that Injun Jim lived mostly in the Tippipah district. No free gold had ever been discovered there, nor much gold of any kind; but Injun Jim certainly brought free gold into Round Butte whenever he wanted grub. It must have been ungodly rich,— five hundred dollars' worth in a ten-pound lard bucket!

The tale held Casey's imagination. He dreamed nights of trailing Injun Jim, and if he'd had any money to outfit for the venture he surely would have gone straight to Nevada and to Round Butte. He told himself that it would take an outsider to furnish the energy for the search. Men who live in a country are the last to see the possibilities lying all around them, Casey said. It was true; he had seen it work out even in himself. Hadn't he driven stage in Cripple Creek country and carried out gold by the hundred-thousand,— gold that might have been his had he not been content to drive stage? Hadn't he lived in gold country all his life, almost, and didn't he know mineral formations as well as many a school-trained expert?

But even dreams of gold fluctuate and grow vague before the small interests of everyday living. Casey hadn't the money just then to quit his job of stage driving and go Indian stalking. It would take money,— a few hundred at least. Casey at that time lacked the price of a ticket to Round Butte. So he had to drive and dream, and his first spurt of saving grew half-hearted as the weeks passed; and then he lost all he had saved in a poker game because he wanted to win enough in one night to make the trip.

However, he went among men with his ears wide open for gossip concerning Injun Jim, and he gleaned bits of information that seemed to confirm what his passenger up in the Yellowstone had told him. He even met a man who knew Injun Jim.

Injun Jim, he was told, had one eye and a bad temper. He had lost his right eye in a fight with soldiers, in the days when Indian fighting was part of a soldier's training. Injun Jim nursed a grudge against the whites because of that eye, and while he behaved himself nowadays, being old and not very popular amongst his own people, it was taken for granted that his trigger finger would never be paralyzed, and that a white man need only furnish him a thin excuse and a fair chance to cover all traces of the killing. Injun Jim would attend to the rest with great zeal.

Stranger still, Casey found that the tale of the lard bucket and the gold was true. This man had once been in the store when Jim arrived for grub. He had taken a piece of the ore in his hands. It was free gold, all right, and it must have come from a district where free gold was scarce as women.

"We've got it figured down to a spot about fifty miles square," the man told Casey. "That old Injun don't travel long trails. He's old. And all Injuns are lazy. They won't go hunting mineral like a white man. They know mineral when they see it and they have good memories and can go to the spot afterwards. Injun Jim prob-ly run across a pocket somewheres when he was hunting. Can't be much of it — he'd bring in more at a time if there was, and be Injun-rich. He's just figurin' on making it hold out long as he lives. 'Tain't worth while trying to find it; there's too much mineral laying around loose in these hills."

Casey stored all that gossip away in the back of his head and through all the ups and downs of the years he never quite forgot it.

CHAPTER XIII

Casey earned a good deal of money, but there are men who are very good at finding original ways of losing money, too. Casey was one. (You should hear Casey unburden himself sometime upon the subject of garages and the tourist trade!) He saved money enough in Patmos to buy two burros and a mule, and what grub and tools the burros could carry. There were no poker games in Patmos, and a discouraged prospector happened along at the right moment, which accounts for it.

In this speed-hungry age Casey had not escaped the warped viewpoint which others assume toward travel. Casey always had craved the sensation of swift moving through space. His old stage horses could tell you tales of that! It was a distinct comedown, buying burros for his venture. That took straight, native optimism and the courage to make the best of things. But he hadn't the price of a Ford, and Casey abhors debt; so he reminded himself cheerfully that many a millionaire would still be poor if he had turned up his nose at burros, sourdough cans and the business end of pick and shovel, and made the deal.

At that, he was better off than most prospectors, he told himself on the night of his purchase. He

CASEY RYAN 131

had the mule, William, to ride. The prospector had assured Casey over and over that William was saddle broke. Casey is too happy-go-lucky, I think. He took the man's word for it and waited until the night before he intended beginning his journey before he gave William a try-out, down in a sandy swale back of the garage. He returned after dark, leading William. Casey had a pronounced limp and an eyetooth was broken short off, about halfway to the gums, and his lip was cut.

"William's saddle broke, all right," he told his neighbor, the proprietor of the Oasis. "I've saw horses broke like that; cow-punchers have fun in the c'rall with 'em Sundays, seein' which one can stay with the saddle three jumps. William don't mind the saddle at all. All he hates is anybody in it." Then he grinned wryly because of his hurt. "No use arguin' with a mule — I used to be too good a walker."

Casey therefore traded his riding saddle for another packsaddle, and collected six coal-oil cans which he cleaned carefully. William was loaded with cans of water, which he seemed to prefer to Casey, though they probably weighed more. The burros waddled off under their loads of beans, flour, bacon, coffee, lard, and a full set of prospector's tools. Casey set his course by the stars and fared forth across the desert, meaning to pass through the lower end of Death Valley by night, on a trail he knew, and so plod up toward the Tippipah country.

He was happy. He owed no man a nickel, he had grub enough to last him three months if he were careful, he had a body tough as seasoned hickory, and he was headed for that great no-man's-land which is the desert. More, he was actually upon the trail of his dream that he had dreamed years before up in the Yellowstone. An old, secretive Indian was going to find his match when Casey Ryan plodded over his horizon and halted beside his fire.

By the way, don't blame me for showing a fondness for gloom and gore when you read the names Casey carried in his mind the next few weeks. Casey crossed Death Valley and the Funeral Mountains — or a spur of them — and headed up toward Spectre Range, going by way of Deadman's Spring, where he filled his water cans. That does not sound cheerful, but Casey was still fairly happy,— though there were moments when he thought seriously of killing William with a rock.

Every morning, without fail, he and William fought every minute from breakfast to starting time. From his actions you would think that William had never seen a pack before, and expected it to bite him fatally if he came within twenty feet of it. You could tell Casey's camp by the manner in which the sagebrush was trampled and the sand scored with small hoofprints in a wide circle around it. But once the battle was lost to William for that day, and Casey had rested and mopped the perspiration off his face and taken a comforting chew of tobacco and relapsed into silence simply because he could think of nothing more to say, William became a pet dog that hazed the two lazy burros along with

CASEY RYAN 133

little nippings on their rumps, and saw to it that they did not stray too far from camp.

Casey strung into Searchlight one evening at dusk and camped on a little knoll behind the town hall, which was open beyond for grazing, and the village dogs were less likely to bother. Searchlight was not on his way, but miles off to one side. Casey made the detour because he had heard a good deal about the place and knew it as a favorite stamping ground of miners and prospectors who sought free gold. Searchlight is primarily a gold camp, you see. He wanted to hear a little more about Injun Jim.

But there had been a murder in Searchlight a dark night or so before his coming, and three suspects were being discussed and championed by their friends. Searchlight was not in the mood for aimless gossip of Indians. Killings had been monotonously frequent, but they usually had daylight and an audience to rob them of mystery. A murder done on a dark night, in the black shadow of an empty dance hall, and accompanied by a piercing scream and the sound of running feet was vastly different.

Casey lingered half a day, bought a few more pounds of bacon and some matches and ten yards of satin ribbon in assorted colors and went his way.

I mention his stop at Searchlight so that those who demand exact geography will understand why Casey journeyed on to Vegas, tramped its hot sidewalks for half a day and then went on by way of Indian Spring to the Tippipah country and his destination. He was following the beaten trail of miners, now that he was in Jim's country, and he was gleaning a little information from every man he met. Not altogether concerning Injun Jim, understand,— but local tidbits that might make him a welcome companion to the old buck when he met him. Casey says you are not to believe story-writers who assume that an Indian is wrapped always in a blanket and inscrutable dignity. He says an Indian is as great a gossip as any old woman, once you get him thawed to the talking point. So he was filling his bag of tricks as he went along.

From Vegas there is what purports to be an automobile road across the desert to Round Butte, and Casey as he walked cursed his burros and William and sighed for his Ford. He was four days traveling to Furnace Lake, which he had made in a matter of hours with his Ford when he first came to Starvation.

He struck Furnace Lake just before dusk one night and pushed the burros out upon it, thinking he would have cool crossing and would start in the morning with the lake behind him, which would be something of a load off his mind. In his heart Casey hated Furnace Lake, and he had good reason. It was a place of ill fortune for him, especially after the sun had left it. He wanted it behind him where he need think no more about it and the grewsome crevice that cut a deep, wide gash two thirds of the way across it through the middle. Casey is not a coward, and he takes most things as a matter of course, but he admits that he has always hated

CASEY RYAN 135

and distrusted Furnace Lake beyond all the dry lakes in Nevada,— and there are many.

He yelled to William, and William nipped the nearest burro into a shambling half trot, and then went out upon the lake, Casey heading across at the widest part so that he would strike his old trail to Starvation Mountain on the other side. From there to the summit he could make it by noon on the morrow, he planned. Which would be the end of his preliminary journey and the beginning of Casey's last drive toward his goal; for from the top of the divide between Starvation Mountain country and that forbidding waste which lies under the calm scrutiny of Furnace Peak he could see the far-off range of the Tippipahs.

He was a mile out on the Lake when he first glimpsed the light. Casey studied it while he walked ahead, leaving no footprints on the hard-baked clay. He had not known that any road followed just under the crest of the ridge that hid Crazy Woman lake, yet the light was plainly that of an automobile moving with speed across the face of the ridge just under the summit.

Away out in the empty land like that you notice little things and think about them and try to understand just what they mean, unless they are perfectly familiar to you. One print of a foot on the trail may betray the lurking presence of a madman, a murderer, a traveling, friendly, desert dweller or the wandering of some one who is lost and dying of thirst and hunger. You like to know which, and you are not satisfied until you do know.

A light moving swiftly along Crazy Woman ridge meant a car, and a car up there meant a road. If there were a road it would probably lead Casey by a shorter route to the Tippipahs. While he looked there came to his ears a roaring, as of some high-powered car traveling under full pressure of gas. The burros followed him, but William lifted his head and brayed tremulously three times in the dark. Casey had never heard him bray before, and the sudden rasping outcry startled him.

He went back and stood for a minute looking at William, who turned tail and started back toward the shore they had left behind them. Casey ran to head him off, yelling threats, and William, in spite of his six water cans — two of them empty — broke into a lope. Casey glanced over his shoulder as he ran and saw dimly that the burros had turned and were coming after him, their ears flapping loosely on their bobbing heads as they trotted. Beyond him, the light still traveled towards the Tippipahs.

Then, with an abruptness that cannot be pictured, everything was blotted out in a great, blinding swirl of dust as the wind came whooping down upon them. It threw Casey as though some one had tripped him. It spun him round and round on his back like an overturned beetle, and then scooted him across the lake's surface flat as a floor. He thought of the Crevice, but there was nothing he could do save hold his head off the ground and his two palms over his face, shielding his nostrils a little from the smother of dust.

Sometimes he was lifted inches from the surface

and borne with incredible swiftness. More than once he was spun round and round until his senses reeled. But all the time he was going somewhere, and I suspect that for once in his life Casey Ryan went fast enough to satisfy him. At last he felt brush sweep past his body, and he knew that he must have been swept to the edge of the lake. He clutched, scratched his hands bloody on the straggly thorns of greasewood, caught in the dark at a more friendly sage and gripped it next the roots. The wind tore at him, howling. Casey flattened his abused body to the hummocky sand and hung on.

Hours later, by the pale stars that peered out breathlessly when the fury of the gale was gone, Casey pulled himself painfully to his feet and looked for the burros and William. Judging by his own experience, they had had a rough time of it and would not go far after the wind permitted them to stop. But as to guessing how far they had been impelled, or in what direction, Casey knew that was impossible. Still, he tried. When the air grew clearer and the surrounding hills bulked like huge shadows against the sky, he saw that he had been blown toward the ridge that guards Crazy Woman lake. His pack animals should be somewhere ahead of him, he thought groggily, and began stumbling along through the brush-covered sand dunes that bordered Furnace Lake for miles.

And then he saw again the light, shining up there just under the crest of the ridge. He was glad the car had escaped, but he reflected that the tricky winds of the desert seldom sweep a large area. Their diabolic fury implies a concentration of force that must of necessity weaken as it flows out away from the center. Up there on the ridge they may not have experienced more than a steady blow.

He walked slowly because of his bruises, and many times he made small detours, thinking that a blotch of shadow off to one side might be his pack train. But always a greasewood mocked him, waving stiff arms at him derisively. In the sage-land distances deceive. A man may walk unseen before your eyes, and a bush afar off may trick you with its semblance to man or beast. Casey finally gave up the hopeless search and headed straight for the light.

It was standing still,— a car facing him with its headlights burning, the distance so great that the two lights glowed as one. "An' it ain't no Ford," Casey decided. "They wouldn't keep the engine runnin' all this time, standin' still. Unless it's one of them old kind with lamps."

I don't suppose you realize, many of you, just what that would mean to a man in the desert country. It is rather hard to define, but the significance would be felt, even by Casey in his present plight. You see, small cars, of the make too famous to be hurt or helped by having its name mentioned in a simple yarn like this, have long been recognized as the proper car for rough trails and no trails. Those who travel the desert most have come to the point of counting "Lizzie" almost as necessary as beans. Wherefore a larger car is nearly always brought in by strangers to the country, who swear solemnly never to repeat the imprudence. A large car, driven by strangers in the land, means hunters, prospectors from the outside brought in by some special tale of hidden wealth,— or just plain simpletons who only want to see what lies over the mountain. There aren't many of the last-named variety up in the Nevada wastes. Even your nature-loving rovers oddly keep pretty much to the beaten trails of other nature lovers, where gas stations and new tires may be found at regular intervals. The Painted Desert, the Petrified Forest, the National Old Trails they explore,— but not the high, wind-swept mesas of Nevada's barren land.

A fear that was not altogether strange to him crept over Casey. It would be just his grinning enemy Ill-luck on his trail again, if that light should prove to be made by men hunting for Injun Jim and his mine. Casey used to feel a sickness in his middle when that thought nagged him, and he felt a growing anger now when he looked at the twinkling glow. He walked a little faster. Now that the fear had come to him, Casey wanted to come up with the men, talk with them, learn their business if they were truthful, or sense their lying if they tried to hide their purpose from him. He must know. If they were seeking Injun Jim, then he must find some way to head them off, circumvent their plans with strategy of his own. He had dreamed too long and too ardently to submit now to interlopers.

So he walked, limping and cursing a little now and then because of his aches. Up a steep slope made heavy with loose sand that dragged at his feet; over the crest and down the other side among rocks and gravel that made harder walking than the sand. Up another steep slope: it was heartbreaking, unending as the toils of a nightmare, but Casey kept on. He was not worried over his own plight; not yet. He believed that William and his burros were somewhere ahead of him, since they could not cling to a bush as he had done and so resist the impetus of that terrific wind. There was a car standing on the ridge toward which he was laboriously making his way. It did not occur to Casey that morning might show him a rather desperate plight.

Yet the morning did just that. Hours before dawn the light had disappeared abruptly, but Casey had no uneasiness over that. It was foolish for them to run down their battery burning lights when they were standing still, he thought. They had not moved off, and he had well in mind the contour of the ridge where they were standing. He would have bet good money that he could walk straight to the car even though darkness hid it from him until he came within hailing distance.

But daylight found him still below the higher slope of the ridge, and Casey was very tired. He had been walking all day, remember, and he had missed his supper because he wanted to eat it with the lake behind him. He did not walk in a straight line. He was too near exhaustion to forge ahead as was his custom. Now he was picking his way carefully so as to shun the washes out of which he must climb, and the rock patches where he would stumble, and the thick brush that would claw at him. He would have given five dollars for a drink of water, but there would be water at the car, he told himself. People were rather particular about carrying plenty of water when they traveled these wastes.

And then he was on the ridge, and his keen eyes were squinted half-shut while he gazed here and there, no foot of exposed land surface escaping that unwinking stare. He took off his hat and wiped his face, and reached mechanically for a chew of tobacco which he always took when perplexed, as if it stimulated thought.

There was no car. There was no road. There was not even a burro trail along that ridge. Yet there had been the lights of a car, and after the lights had been extinguished Casey had listened rather anxiously for sound of the motor and had heard nothing at all. The most powerful, silent-running car on the market would have made some noise in traveling through that sand and up and down the washes that seamed the mountain side. Casey would have heard it — he had remarkably keen hearing.

"And that's darn funny," he muttered, when he was perfectly sure that there was no car, that there could never have been a car on that trackless ridge. "That's mighty damn funny! You can ask anybody."

CHAPTER XIV

Other things, however, were not so funny to Casey as he stood staring down over the vast emptiness. There was no sign of his pack train, and without it he would be in sorry case indeed. He thought of the manner in which the tornado had whirled him round and round. Caught in a different set of gyrations and then borne out from the center — flung out would come nearer it — the burros and William might have been carried in any direction save his own. Into that gruesome Crevice, for instance. They had not been more than a mile from the Crevice when the storm struck.

He glanced across to Barren Butte, rising steeply from the farther end of the lake. But he did not think of going to the mine up there, except to tell himself that he'd rot on the desert before he ever asked there for help. He had his reasons, you remember. A man like Casey can face humiliation from men much easier than he can face a woman who had misjudged him and scorned him. Unless, of course, he has a million dollars in his pocket and knows that she knows it.

Having discarded Barren Butte from his plans — rather, having declined to consider it at all — he knew that he must find his supplies, or he must find water somewhere in the Crazy Woman hills. The prospect was not bright, for he had never heard any one mention water there.

He rested where he was for awhile and watched the slope for the pack animals; more particularly for William and the water cans. He could shoot rabbits and live for days, if he had a little water, but he had once tried living on rabbit meat broiled without salt, and he called it dry eating, even with water to wash it down. Without water he would as soon fast and let the rabbits live.

A dark speck moving in the sage far down the slope caught his eyes, and he got up and peered that way eagerly. He started down to meet it hopefully, feeling certain that his present plight would soon merge into a mere incident of the trail. Sure enough, when he had walked for half an hour he saw that it was William, browsing toward him and limping when he moved.

But William was bare as the back of Casey's hand. There was no pack, no coal-oil cans of water; only the halter and lead rope, that dangled and caught on brush and impeded William's limping progress. I suppose even miserable mules like company, for William permitted Casey to walk up and take him by the halter rope. William had a badly skinned knee which gave him the limp, and his right ear was broken close to his head so that the structure which had been his pride dropped over his eye like a wet sunbonnet.

Casey swore a little and started back along William's tracks to find the water cans. He followed a winding, purposeless trail that never showed the track of burros, and after an hour or so he came upon the pack and the cans. Evidently the water supply had suffered in the wind, for only four cans were with the blankets and pack saddle.

William had felt his pack slipping, Casey surmised, and had proceeded to divest himself of the incumbrance in the manner best known to mules. Having kicked himself out of it, he had undoubtedly discovered a leaking can — supposing the cans had escaped thus far — and had battered them with his heels until they were all leaking copiously. William had saved what he could.

Casey read the whole story in the sand. The four cans were bent with gaping seams, and their sides were scored with the prints of William's hoofs. In a corner of one of them Casey found a scant half-cup of water, which he drank greedily. It could no more than ease for a moment his parched throat; it could not satisfy his thirst.

After that he led William back along the trail until the mounting sun warned him that he was making no headway on his journey to the Tippipahs, and that with no tracks in sight he had small hope of tracing the burros.

It was sundown again before he gave up hope, and Casey's thirst was a demon within him. He had wasted a day, he told himself grimly. Now it was going to be a fight.

Through the day he had mechanically studied the geologic formation of those hills before him, and he had decided that the chance for water there was too slight to make a search worth while. He would push on toward the Tippipahs. *Pah,* he knew, meant water in the Indian tongue. He did not know what *Tippi* signified, but since Indians lived in the Tippipah range he was assured that the water was drinkable. So he got stiffly to his feet, studied again the darkling skyline, sent a glance up at the first stars, and turned his face and William's resolutely toward the Tippipahs.

He had applied first aid to William's knee in the form of chewed tobacco, which if it did no more at least discouraged the pestering flies. Now he collected a ride for his pay. He had reasoned that William was probably subdued to the point of permitting the liberty, and that he had other things to think of more important than protecting his mulish dignity. Casey guessed right. William merely switched his tail pettishly, as mules will, and went on picking his way through brush and rocks along the ridge.

It was perhaps nine o'clock when Casey saw the light. William also spied it and stopped still, his long left ear pointed that way, his broken right ear dropping over his eye. William lifted his nose and brayed as if he were tearing loose all his vitals and the operation hurt like the mischief. Casey kicked him in the flanks and urged him on. It must be a camp fire, Casey thought. He did not connect it with that moving light he had seen the night before; that phantom car was a mystery which he would probably never solve, and in Casey's opinion it had nothing to do with a camp fire that twinkled upon a distant hilltop.

From the look of it, Casey judged that it was perhaps eight miles off,— possibly less. But there was a rocky canyon or two between them, and William was lame and Casey was too exhausted to walk more than half a mile before he must lie down and own himself whipped. Casey Ryan had never done that for a man, and he did not propose to do it for Nature. He thought that William ought to have enough stamina to make the trip if he were given time enough. And at the last, if William gave out, then Casey would manage somehow to walk the rest of the way. It all depended upon giving William time enough.

You know, mules are the greatest mind readers in the world. I have always heard that, and now Casey swears that it is so. William immediately began taking his time. Casey told me that a turtle starting nose to nose with William would have had to pull in his feet and wait for him every half mile or so. William must have been very thirsty, too.

The light burned steadily, hearteningly. Whenever they crawled to high ground where a view was possible, Casey saw it there, just under a certain star which he had used for a marker at first. And whenever William saw the light he brayed and tried to swing around and go the other way. But Casey would not permit that, naturally. Nor did he wonder why William acted so queerly. You never wonder why a mule does things; you just fight it out and are satisfied if you win, and let it go at that.

Casey does not remember clearly the details of that night. He knows that during the long hours

William balked at a particularly steep climb, and that Casey was finally obliged to get off and lead the way. It established an unfortunate precedent, for William refused to let Casey on again, and Casey was too weak to mount in spite of William. They compromised at last; that is, they both walked.

The light went out. Moreover, Casey's star that he had used to mark the spot moved over to the west and finally slid out of sight altogether. But Casey felt sure of the direction and he kept going doggedly toward the point where the light had been. He says there wasn't a rod where a snail couldn't have outrun him, and when the sky streaked red and orange and the sun came up, he stood still and looked for a camp, and when he saw nothing at all but bare rock and bushes of the kind that love barrenness, he crawled under the nearest shade, tied William fast to the bush and slept. You don't realize your thirst so much when you are asleep, and you are saving your strength instead of wearing it out in the hot sun. He remained there until the sun was almost out of sight behind a high peak. Then he got up, untied William, mounted him without argument from either, and went on, keeping to the direction in which he had seen the light.

Even the little brown mule was having trouble now. He wavered, he picked his footing with great care when a declivity dipped before him; he stopped every few yards and rested when he was making a climb. As for Casey, he managed to hold himself on the narrow back of William, but that was all. He understood perfectly that the next twenty-four hours would tell the story for him and for William. He had a sturdy body however and a sturdy brain that had never weakened its hold on facts. So he clung to his reason and pushed fear away from him and said doggedly that he would go forward as long as he could crawl or William could carry him, and he would die or he would not die, as Fate decided for him. He wondered, too, about the camp whose fire he had seen.

Then he saw the light. This time it burned suddenly clear and large and very bright, away off to the left of him where he had by daylight noticed a bare shale slide. The light seemed to stand in the very center of the slide, no more than a mile away.

William stopped when Casey pulled on the reins he had fashioned from the lead rope, and turned stiffly so that he faced the light. Casey kicked him gently with his heels to urge him forward, for in spite of what his reason told him about the shale slide his instinct was to go straight to the light. But William began to shiver and tremble, and to swing slowly away. Casey tried to prevent it, but the mule came out in William. He laid his good ear flat along his neck as far as it would go, and took little, nipping steps until he had turned with his tail to the light. Then he thrust his fawn-colored muzzle to the stars and brayed and brayed, his good ear working like a pump handle as he tore the sounds loose from his vitals.

Casey cursed him in a whisper, having no voice left. He kicked William in the flanks, having no other means of coercion at hand. But kicking never yet altered the determination of a mule, and cursing a mule in a whisper is like blowing your breath against the sail of a becalmed sloop. William kept his tail toward the light, and furthermore he momentarily drew his tail farther and farther from that spot. Now and then he would turn his head and glance back, and immediately increase his pace a little. He was long past the point where he had strength to trot, but he could walk, and he did walk and carry Casey on his back, still whispering condemnation.

They did not travel all night. Casey looked at the Big Dipper and judged it was midnight when they stopped on the brink of a deep canyon, halted there in William's sheer despair because the light appeared suddenly on the high point of a hill directly ahead of them. William's voice was gone like Casey's, so that he, too, cursed in a whisper with a spasmodic indrawing of ribs and a wheezing in his throat.

When it was plain that the mule had stopped permanently, Casey slid off William's back and lay down without knowing or caring much whether he would ever get up again. He said he wasn't hungry — much; but his mouth was too full of tongue, he added grimly.

He lay and watched through half-closed, staring eyes the light that mocked him so. His dulling senses told him that it was no camp fire, nor any light made by human hands. He did not know what it was. He didn't care any more. William crumpled up and lay down beside him, breathing heavily. It was getting close to the end of things.

Casey knew it, and he thinks William knew it too.

The sun found them there and forced Casey to move. He sat up painfully, the fight to live not yet burned out of him, and gazed dully at the forbidding hills that closed around him like great, naked rock demons watching to see him die for want of the things they withheld. Where he remembered the light to have been when last he saw it was bleak, bare rock. It was a devil's light and there was nothing friendly or human about it.

He looked down into the canyon which William had refused to enter. A faint interest revived within him because of a patch of green. Trees,— but they might easily be junipers which will grow in dry canyons as readily, it would seem, as in any other. He kept looking, because green was a great relief from the monotonous gray and black and brown of the hills. It seemed to him after awhile that he saw a small splotch of dead white.

In the barren lands two things will show white in the distance; a white horse and a tent of white canvas. Casey shifted his position and squinted long at the spot, then got up slowly with the help of a bush and took William by the rope. William was on his feet, standing with head dropped, apparently half asleep. Casey knew that William was simply waiting until he could no longer stand.

Together they wabbled down the sloping canyon side and over a grassy bottom to the trees, which were indeed juniper trees, but thriftier looking than their brethren of the dry places. There was water, for William smelled it at last and hurried forward with more briskness than Casey could muster, eager though he was to reach the tent he saw standing there under the biggest juniper.

Beside the tent was a water bucket of bright, new tin. A white granite dipper stood in it. Casey drank sparingly and stopped when he would have given all he ever possessed in the world to have gone on drinking until he could hold no more. But he was not yet crazy with the thirst. So he stopped drinking, filled a white granite basin and soused his head again and again, sighing with sheer ecstasy at the drip of water down his back and chest. After a little he drank two swallows more, put down the dipper and went into the tent.

CHAPTER XV

We can all remember certain experiences that fill us with incredulity even while we admit that the facts could be proved before a jury of twelve men. So Casey Ryan, having lost his outfit and come so near to death that he could barely keep his feet under him, walked into a tent and stood there thinking it couldn't be true.

A folding camp chair stood near the opening, and Casey sat down from sheer weakness while he looked about him. The tent was a twelve-by-fourteen, which is a bit larger than one usually carries in a pack outfit. It had a canvas floor soiled in strips where the most walking had been done, but white under table and beds, which proved its newness. Casey was not accustomed to seeing tents floored with canvas, and he stared at it for a full half-minute before his eyes went to other things.

There was a folding camp table of the kind shown in the window display of sporting-goods stores, but which seasoned campers find too wobbly for actual comfort. The varnish still shone on legs and braces, which helped to prove its newness. There was a two-burner oil stove with an enamel-rimmed oven that was distinctly out of place in that country and yet harmonized perfectly with the tent and furnishings. The dishes were white enamel or aluminum, and there were boxes piled upon boxes, the labels proclaiming canned things too expensive for ordinary eating. Two spring cots with new blankets and white-cased pillows stood against the tent wall, and beneath each cot sat two yellow pigskin suitcases with straps and brass buckles. They would have been perfectly natural in a Pullman sleeper, but even in his present stress Casey snorted disdainfully at sight of them here.

Things were tumbled about in the disorder of inexperienced campers, but everything was very new and clean except an array of dishes on the table, which told Casey that one man had eaten at least three meals without washing his dishes or putting away his surplus of food. Casey had eaten nothing at all after that one toasted rabbit which he had choked down on the evening when he gave up hope of finding the burros. He got up and staggered stiffly to the table and picked up a piece of burned biscuit, hard as flint.

While he mumbled a fragment of that he looked into various half-filled cans, setting them one by one in a compact group on the table corner; which was habit rather than conscious thought. Poisonous ptomaine lurked in every one of them, which was a shame, since he had to discard half a can of preserved peaches, half a can of roast beef, half a can of asparagus tips, a can of chicken soup scarcely touched and two thirds of a can of sweet potatoes. He salvaged a can of ripe olives which he thought was good, a can of India relish and a can of sweet gherkins (both of the fifty-seven varieties). You will see what I meant when I spoke of expensive camp food.

There was cold coffee in a nickel percolater, and Casey poured himself a cup, knowing well the risk of eating much just at first. It was while he was unscrewing the top of the glass jar that held the sugar that he first noticed the paper. It was folded and thrust into the sugar jar, and Casey pulled it out and held it crumpled in his hand while he sweetened and drank the coffee, forcing himself to take it slowly. When the cup was empty to the last drop he went over and sat down on the edge of a spring cot and unfolded the note. What he read surprised him a great deal and puzzled him more. I leave it to you to judge why.

"I saw it again last night in a different place. The last horse died yesterday down the canyon. You can have the outfit. I'm going to beat it out of here while the going's good. FRED."

"That's mighty damn funny," Casey muttered thickly. "You can — ask —" He lay back luxuriously, with his head on the white pillow and closed his eyes. The reaction from struggling to live had set in with the assurance of his safety. He slept heavily, refreshingly.

He awoke to the craving for food, and immediately started a small fire outside and boiled coffee in a nice new aluminum pail that held two quarts and had an ornamental cover. The oil stove he dismissed from his mind with a snort of contempt. And because nearly everything he saw was catalogued in his mind as a luxury, he opened cans somewhat extravagantly and dined off strange, delectable foods to which his palate was unaccustomed. He still thought it was mighty queer, but that did not impair his appetite.

Afterwards he went out to look after William, remembering that horses were said to have died in this place. William was almost within kicking distance of the spring, as if he meant to keep an eye upon the water supply even though that involved browsing off brush instead of wandering down to good grass below the camp.

Casey knelt stiffly and drank from the spring, laving his face and head afterward as if he never would get enough of the luxury of being wet and cool. He rose and stood looking at William for a few minutes, then took the lead rope and tied him to a juniper that stood near the spring. The note had said that the last horse died down the canyon, the implication of mystery lying heavy behind the words.

Casey went back to the tent and read the note through again twice, studying each word as if he hoped to twist some added information out of it. It sounded as though the writer had expected his partner back from some trip and had left the note for him, since he had not considered it necessary to explain what it was that he had seen again in a different place. Casey wondered if it might not have been that strange light which he himself had followed. Whatever it was, the fellow had not liked it. His going had all the earmarks of flight.

Well, then, why had the last horse died down the canyon? Casey decided that he would go and see, though he was not hankering for exercise that day. He took a long drink of water, somewhat shamefacedly filled a new canteen that lay on a pile of odds and ends near the tent door, and started down the canyon. It couldn't be far, but he might want a drink before he got back, and Casey had had enough of thirst.

He was not long in finding the horse that had died, and in fact all the horses that had died. There had been four, and the manner of their death was not in the least mysterious. They had been staked out to graze in a luxurious patch of loco weed, which is reason enough why any horse should die.

Of course, no man save an unmitigated tenderfoot would picket a horse on loco, which looks very much like wild peavine and is known the West over as the deadliest weed that grows. A little of it mixed with a diet of grass will drive horses and cattle insane, and there is no authentic case of recovery, that I ever heard, once the infection is complete. A lot of it will kill,— and these poor beasts had actually been staked out to graze upon it, I suppose because it looked nice and green, and the horses liked it.

The performance matched very well the enamel-trimmed oil stove and the tinned dainties and the expensive suitcases. Casey went back to camp feeling as though he had stumbled upon a picnic of feeble-minded persons. He wondered what in hell two men of such a type could be doing out there, a hundred miles and more from an ice-cream soda and a barber's chair. He wondered too how "Fred" had expected to get himself across that hundred miles and more of dry desert country. He must certainly be afoot, and the camp itself showed no sign of an emergency outfit having been assembled from its furnishings.

Casey made sure of that, inspecting first the bedding and food and then the cooking utensils. Everything was complete — lavishly so — for two men who loved comfort. Even their sweaters were there; and Casey knew they must have discovered that the nights can be cool even though the days are hot, in that altitude. And there were two canteens of the size usually carried by hikers.

Casey was so worried that he could not properly enjoy his supper of *pâté de foi gras* and crackers, with pork and beans, plum pudding — eaten as cake — and spiced figs and coffee. That night he turned over on his spring-cot bed as often as if he had been lying on nettles, and when he did sleep he dreamed horribly.

Next morning he set out with William and an emergency camp outfit to trace if he could the missing men. The great outdoors of Nevada is not kind to such as these, and Casey had too lately suffered to think with easy-going optimism that they would manage somehow. They would die if they were left to shift for themselves, and Casey could not pretend that he did not know it.

But there was a difficulty in rescuing them, just as there had been in rescuing the burros. Casey could not find their tracks, and so could not follow them. He and William hunted the canyon from top to bottom and ranged far out on the valley floor without discovering anything that could be called the track of a man. Which was strange, too, in a country where footprints are held for a long, long while by the soil,— as souvenirs of man's passing, perhaps.

So it transpired that Casey at length returned to the new tent just below the spring in the nameless canyon beyond Crazy Woman Lake. Chipmunks had invaded the place and feasted upon an opened package of sweet crackers, but otherwise the tent had been left inviolate. Neither Fred nor his partner had returned. Wherefore Casey opened more cans and " made himself to home," as he naively put it.

He was impatient to continue his journey, but since he had nothing of his own except William, he meant to beg or buy a few things from this camp, if either of the owners showed up. Meantime he could be comfortable, since it is tacitly understood in the open land that a wayfarer may claim hospitality of any man, with or without that man's knowledge. He is expected to keep the camp clean, to leave firewood and to take nothing away with him except what is absolutely necessary to insure his getting safely to the next stopping place. Casey knew well the law, and he busied himself in setting the camp in order while he waited.

But when five days and nights had slipped into history and he and William were still in sole pos-

CASEY RYAN 159

session, Casey began to take another viewpoint. Fred might possibly have left in a flying machine. The partner might have decamped permanently before Fred lost his nerve. Several things might have happened which would leave this particular camp and contents without a claimant. Casey studied the matter for awhile and then pulled the four suitcases from beneath the cots and proceeded to investigate. The first one that he opened had a note folded and addressed to Fred. Casey read it through without the slightest compunction. The handwriting was different from that of the first note, hurried and scrawly, the words connected with faint lines. Here is what Fred's partner had written:

"DEAR FRED: Don't blame me for leaving you. A man that carries the grouch you do don't need company. I'm fed up on solitude, and I don't like the feel of things here. My staying won't help your lung a damn bit and if you want anything you can hunt up the men that carry the light. Maybe they are the ones that are killing off the horses. Anyway, you can wash your own dishes from now on. It will do you good. If I had of known you were the crab you are I'll say I would never have come. You are welcome to my share of the outfit. I hope some one shoots me and puts me out of my misery quick if I ever show symptoms of wanting to camp out again. I am going now because if I stayed I'd change your map for you so your own looking glass wouldn't know you. I'll say you are some nut.
"ART."

Casey had to take a fresh chew of tobacco before

his brain would settle down and he could think clearly. Then he observed that it was a damn funny combination and you could ask anybody. After that he began to realize that he was heir to a fine assortment of canned delicacies and an oil stove and four suitcases filled, he hoped, with good clothes. Not omitting possession of two spring cots and several pairs of high-grade blankets, and two sweaters and Lord knows what all.

Those suitcases were enough to make any man sit and bite his nails, wondering if he were crazy. Fred and Art had evidently fitted their wardrobe to their ideas of a summer camp with dancing pavilion and plenty of hammocks in the immediate neighborhood. There were white flannel trousers and white canvas shoes and white silk socks, and fine ties and handkerchiefs and things. There were striped silk shirts which made Casey grin and think how tickled Injun Jim would be with them,— or one or two of them; Casey had no intention of laying them all on the altar of diplomacy. There was an assortment of apparel in those suitcases that would qualify any man as porch hound at Del Monte. And Casey Ryan, if you please, had fallen heir to the lot!

He dressed himself in white flannels with a silk shirt of delf blue and pale green stripes, and wished that there was a looking-glass in camp large enough to reflect all of him at once. Then, because his beard stubble did not harmonize, he shaved with one of the safety razors he found.

After that he sorted and packed a careful wardrobe, and stored strange food into two canvas kyacks. And the next evening he tied the tent flaps carefully and fared forth with William to find the camp of Injun Jim and see if his dream would come true.

CHAPTER XVI

You may not believe this next incident. I know I did not, when Casey told me about it,— but now I am not so sure. Casey said that the light appeared again, that night, moving slowly along the lip of the canyon like a man with a large lantern. There was a full moon, which had made him decide to travel at night on account of the heat while the sun was up. But the moon did not reveal the cause of the light, though the canyon crest was plainly visible to him.

William swung away from that light and walked rather briskly in the other direction, and Casey did not argue with him. So they headed almost due west and kept going. It seemed to Casey once or twice that the light followed them; but he could not be sure.

Two full nights he journeyed, and on both nights he had the light behind him. Once it came up swiftly to within a mile or so of him and William, and stopped there for awhile and then disappeared. Casey camped rather early and slept, and took the trail again in the morning. Night travel was getting on his nerves.

All that day he walked and toward evening, with thunder heads piling high above the Tippipahs, he came upon a small herd of Indian ponies feeding out from the mouth of a wide gulch. He knew they were Indian ponies by their size, their variegated colors, and their general unkemptness. They presently spied him and went galloping off up the gulch, and Casey followed until he spied a thin bluish ribbon of smoke wavering up toward the slate-black clouds.

He made camp just out of sight around a point of rocks from the smoke, stretching the canvas tarp which had floored the tent to make shelter between boulders. He changed his clothes, dressing himself carefully in the white flannel trousers, blue-and-green striped silk shirt, tan belt, white shoes and his old Stetson tilted over his right eye at the characteristic Casey angle. He was taking it for granted that an Indian camp lay under that smoke, and he knew Indians. Inquisitiveness would shut them up as effectively as poking a stick at a clam; but there were ways of coaxing their interest, nevertheless, and when an Indian is curious you have the trumps in your own hand and it will be your own fault if you lose.

Casey's manner therefore was extremely preoccupied when he led a suddenly limping William up the gulch and past a stone hut with a patched tepee alongside it. A lean squaw stood erect before the tepee and regarded him fixedly from under the shade of a mahogany-colored hand, and when Casey came closer she stooped and ducked out of sight like a prairie dog diving into its burrow. Casey paid no attention to that. He knew without being told that he was under close scrutiny from eyes unseen; which was what he desired and had prepared for.

The spring, as he had guessed, was above the camp. He threw a rock at two yammering curs that rushed out at him, and drove them back with Caseyish curses. Then he watered William at the trampled spring, made himself a smoke, and went back down the gulch. Opposite the tepee the squaw stood beside the trial. Casey grinned amiably and said hello.

"Yo' ketchum 'bacco? My man, him heap sick. Mebby die. Likeum 'bacco, him." The squaw muttered it as if she would rather not speak, but had been commanded to beg tobacco from the stranger.

"Sure, I got tobacco!" Casey's tone was a bit more friendly than before. He pulled a small red can from his shirt pocket, hesitated and then tied William to a bush. "Too bad your man sick. Mebby I can help him. He in here?"

The squaw gestured dumbly, and Casey stooped and went into the tepee.

Inside it was so dark that he stood still just within the opening to get his bearings. This happened to be very good form in Indian society, and we will assume that Casey lost nothing by the pause. He dimly saw that a few blankets lay untidily against the tepee wall and that an old Indian was stretched upon them, watching Casey with one black eye, the other lid lying in sunken folds across the socket. Casey was for once in his life speechless. He had not expected to walk straight into the camp of Injun Jim. He had thought that of course he would have to go on to Round Butte and glean information there, perhaps; if he were exceptionally lucky he would meet Indians who would tell him what he wanted to know. But here was a one-eyed buck, and he was old, and he lived in the Tippipahs,—Injun Jim by all description.

"Your squaw says you want tobacco." Casey advanced and held out the red can. He knew better than to waste words, especially in the beginning. Indians are peculiar; you must approach them by not seeming to approach at all.

The old fellow grunted and turned the can over and over in clawlike hands, and said he wanted a match and a paper. Casey went farther; he rolled a cigarette and gave it to him and then rolled one for himself. They smoked, there in that unsavory tepee, saying nothing at all. Casey had achieved the first part of his dream; he was making friends with Injun Jim.

Later he went down to his own camp, leading William. It was hard to wait and watch for the proper moment to broach the subject that filled his mind, and then induce the old Indian to talk. Casey was beginning to understand why no one had wormed the secret from Jim. When you are hundreds of miles and many months distant from a problem it is easy to decide that you will do so and so, and handle the matter differently from the bungling men you have heard about. To find Injun Jim and get him to tell where his gold mine was had seemed fairly easy to Casey when he was driving stage elsewhere, and could only think about it. But when he sat on his haunches in the tepee, smoking with Injun Jim and conversing intermittently of such vital things as the prospect of rain that night, and the enforced delay in his journey because his pack mule was lame, speaking of gold mines in a properly disinterested and casual manner was not at all easy.

However, Casey ate a very hearty supper and went to bed studying the problem of somehow winning the old fellow's gratitude. Morning did not bring a solution, as it properly should have done, but he ransacked his pack, chose a small glass jar of blackberry jam and a little can of maple syrup, fortified himself with another red can of tobacco and went up to the camp, hoping for a streak of good luck. As for medicine, he hadn't a drop, and if he had he did not know for certain what ailed Injun Jim. He thought it was just old age and general cussedness.

Injun Jim ate the jam, using a deadly looking knife and later his fingers, when the jam got low in the jar. When he had finished that he opened the can and drank the maple syrup just as he would have drunk whisky,— with a relish. He smoked Casey's tobacco in the stone pipe which the squaw brought him and appeared fairly well satisfied with life. But he did not talk much, and what he did say was of no importance whatever. Not once did he mention gold mines.

Casey went back to camp and swore at William as he counted his cans of luxuries. He did not realize that he had established a dangerous precedent, but when he led William up to water, meaning to pass by the camp without stopping, the squaw halted him on his way back and told him briefly that her man wanted him.

Injun Jim did not want Casey; he wanted more jam. Casey went back to camp and got another can, this time of strawberry, and in a spirit of peevishness added a small tin of the liver paste that had caused him a night's discomfort. He took them to the tepee, and Injun Jim ate the complete contents of both cans and seemed disgruntled afterwards; so much so that he would not talk at all but smoked in brooding silence, staring with his one malevolent eye at the stained wall of the tepee.

An hour later he began to move himself restlessly in the blanket and to mutter Piute words, the full meaning of which Casey did not grasp. But he would not answer when he was spoken to, so Casey went back to his camp. And that night Injun Jim was very sick.

Next day however he was sufficiently recovered to want more jam. Casey filled his pockets with small cans and doled them out one by one and gossiped artfully while he watched Injun Jim eat pickles, India relish and jelly with absolute, inscrutable impartiality. Casey felt sympathetic qualms in his own stomach just from watching the performance, but he was talking for a gold mine and he did not stop.

" You know Willow Pete? " he asked garrulously. " Big, tall man. Drinks whisky all the time. Willow Pete found a gold mine two moons ago. He's rich now. Got a big barrel of whisky. Got silk shirts like this —" he plucked at his own silken sleeve "— got lots of jam all the time. Every day drinks whisky and eats jam."

"Hunh!" Injun Jim ran his forefinger dexterously around the inside of a jelly glass and licked the finger with the nonchalance of a two-year-old. "Hunh. Got heap big gol' mine, me. No can go ketchum two year, mebby. I dunno. Feet no damn good for walk. Back no damn good for ride. No ketchum gol' long time now."

Casey took a chew of tobacco. This was getting to the point he had been aiming for, and he needed his wits working at top speed.

"Well, if you got a gold mine, you can eat jam all the time. Drink whisky, too," he added, hushing his conscience peremptorily. "If you've got a white man that's your friend, he might take your gold to town and buy whisky and jam."

Injun Jim considered, his finger searching for more jelly. "White man no good for Injun, mebby. I dunno. Ketchum gol', mebby no givum. Tell all white mans. Heap mans come. White man horses eat grass. Drink all water. Shootum deer, shootum rabbit, shootum all damn time. Make big house. Heap noise all time. No place for Injuns no more. No good."

"White man not all same, Jim. One white man maybe good friend. Help get gold, give you half. You buy lots of jam, lots of whisky, lots of silk shirts, have good time." Casey looked at him straight. He could do it, because he meant what he said; even the whisky, I regret to say.

Injun Jim accepted a cigarette and smoked it,

saying never a word. Casey smoked the mate to it and waited, trying to hide how his fingers trembled. Injun Jim turned himself painfully on the blankets and regarded Casey steadily with his one suspicious eye. Casey met the look squarely.

"You got more shirt?" Jim's finger pointed at the blue and green stripes. "Yo' got more jam? You bringum. Heap sick, me, mebby die. Me no takeum gol' me die. No wantum, me die. Yo' mebby good man. I dunno. Me ketchum heap jam, ketchum heap silk shirt, ketchum heap 'bacco, heap whisky, mebby me tellum you where ketchum gol' mine. Me die, yo' heap rich —"

He turned suddenly, lifted his right arm and sent his knife swishing through the air. It sliced its way through the tepee wall and hung there quivering, caught by the hilt. Injun Jim called out vicious, Piute words. "Hahnaga!" he commanded fiercely. "Hahnaga!"

The lean old squaw came meekly, stood just within the tepee while her lord spat words at her. She answered apathetically in Piute and backed out. Presently she returned, driving before her a young squaw whom Casey had not before seen. The young squaw was holding a hand upon her other arm, and Casey saw blood between her fingers. The young squaw was not particularly meek. She stood there sullenly while Injun Jim berated her in the Indian tongue, and once she muttered a retort that made the old man's fingers go groping over the blankets for a weapon; whereat the young squaw laughed contemptuously and went out, sending

Casey a side glance and a fleeting smile as full of coquetry as ever white woman could employ.

The interruption silenced the old buck upon the subject of gold. Casey sat there and chewed tobacco and waited, schooling his impatience as best he could. Injun Jim muttered in Piute, or lay with his one eye closed. But Casey knew that he did not sleep; his thin lips were drawn too tense for slumber. So he waited.

Injun Jim opened his eye suddenly, looked all around the tepee and then stared fixedly at Casey. "Young squaw no good. Heap much white talk. Stealum gol' mine, mebby. I dunno." He gestured for his knife, and Casey got it for him. Injun Jim fondled it evilly.

"Bimeby killum. Mebby. I dunno. Yo' ketchum jam, ketchum shirt—how many jam yo' ketchum?"

Casey meditated awhile. He had not planned an exclusive jam diet for Injun Jim, therefore his supply was getting low. But at the tenderfoot camp was much more, enough to last Injun Jim to the border of the happy hunting grounds,— if he did not loiter too long upon the way. There was no telling how long Injun Jim would be able to eat jam, but Casey was a good gambler.

"If I go get a lot more, and get silk shirts — six," he counted with his fingers, "you tell me where your gold mine is."

"Yo' bringum heap jam, bringum shirt. Me tellum." His one eye was bright. "Yo' bringum jam. Yo' bringum shirt. Yo' giveum me." He patted the bare dirt beside the blankets, signifying that he wanted the jam and shirts there, within reach of his hand. He even twisted his cruel old lips into a smile. "Me tellum. Me shakeum hand."

He held out his left hand and Casey clasped it soberly, though he wanted to jump up and crack his heels together,— as he confided afterwards. Injun Jim laid the blade of his knife across the clasped hands.

"Yo' lie me, yo' die quick. Injun god biteum. Mebby snake. I dunno. How long yo' ketchum heap jam, heap shirt?"

Now that he knew the way, Casey had in mind a certain short-cut that would subtract two days from the round trip. He held up his hand, fingers spread, and got up. Then he thought of the threat and added one of his own.

"I've got a God myself, Jim. You lie about that gold mine and the jam'll choke yuh to death. You can ask anybody."

Casey went out and straightway packed for the journey. Fate, he told himself, was playing partners with him. I don't suppose Casey, even in his most happy-go-lucky mood, had ever been quite so content with life as when he returned to the camp of the tenderfeet for a mule load of jam and silk shirts. Trading an old muzzle-loading shotgun to an Indian chief for the future site of a great city could not have seemed more of a bargain in the days of our forefathers.

CHAPTER XVII

He made the trip almost half a day sooner than he had promised and went straight up to Injun Jim's camp with his load. He was whistling all the way up the canyon to the tepee; but then he stopped.

Inside the hut was the sound of wailing. Casey tried not to guess what that meant. He tied William and went to the door of the tepee.

The young squaw came from within and stood just before the opening, regarding Casey with that maddening, Indian immobility so characteristic of the race. She did not speak, though Casey waited for fully two minutes; nor did she move aside to let him go in. Casey grinned disarmingly.

"Me ketchum heap jam for Injun Jim. Heap silk shirts. Me go tellum," he said.

"Are those they?" the young squaw inquired calmly, and pointed to William. Casey jumped. Any man would, hearing that impeccable sentence issue from the lips of a squaw with a blanket over her head.

"Uh-huh," he gulped.

"My father is dead. He died yesterday from eating too much pickles that you gave him. I should like to have what you have brought to give him. I should thank you for the silk shirts. I can fix them

CASEY RYAN 173

so that I can wear them. I will talk to you pretty soon about that gold mine. I know where it is. I have helped my father bring the gold away. My father would not tell you if you gave him all the jam and all the silk in the world. My father was awful mean. I thought he would maybe kill you and that is why I listened beside the tepee. I wished to protect you because I know that you are a good man. Will you give me the silk shirts and the jam?"

She smiled then, and Casey saw that she had a gold tooth in front, which further demonstrated how civilized she was.

"You will excuse the way I am dressed. I have to dress so that I would please my father. He was very mean with me all the time. He did not like me because I have gone to school and got a fine educating. He wanted me to be Indian. But I knew that my father is a chief and that makes me just what you would say a princess, and I wished to learn how to be educate like all white ladies. So I took some gold from my father's mine and I spent the money for going to school. My name," she added impressively, "is Lucy Lily. What is your name?"

"Mr. — Casey Ryan," he stuttered, floundering in the mental backwash left by this flood of amazing eloquence.

"I like that name. I think I will have you for my friend. Do not talk to my mother, Hahnaga. She is crazy. She tells lies all the time about me. She does not like me because I have went to school and got a fine educating. She is mad all the time when she sees that I am not like her. Now you give me the silks. I will put on a pretty dress. My father is dead now and I can do what I wish to do; I am not afraid of my mother. My mother does not know where to find the gold mine. I am the only one who knows."

Casey is a simple soul, too trustful by far. He was embarrassed by the arch smile which Lucy Lily gave him, and he wished vaguely that she was the blanket squaw she looked to be. But it never occurred to Casey that there might be a wily purpose behind her words. He unpacked William and gave her the things he had brought for Injun Jim, and returned with his camp outfit to the spring to think things over while he boiled himself a pot of coffee and fried bacon.

Lucy Lily appeared like an unwarranted vision before him. Indeed, Casey likened her coming to a nightmare. Casey no longer wondered why Injun Jim insisted upon Indian dress for Lucy Lily.

Now she wore a red silk skirt much spotted with camp grease. A three-cornered tear in the side had been sewed with long stitches and coarse white thread, and even Casey was outraged by the unworkmanlike job. She had on one of the silk shirts, which happened to be striped in many shades, none of which harmonized with the basic color of the skirt. She also wore two cheap necklaces whose luster had long since faded, and her hair was coiled on top of her head and adorned with three combs containing many white glass settings. Her face was powdered thickly to the point of her jaws, with very red cheekbones and very red lips. She wore once-white slippers with French heels much run over at the side and dirty white silk stockings with great holes in the heels. I must add that the shirt was too narrow in the bust, so that her arms bulged and there were gaping spaces between the buttons. And for a belt she wore a wide blue ribbon very much creased and soiled, as if she had used it for a long while as a hair bow.

She sat down upon a rock and watched Casey distractedly bungle his cooking. She must have had a great deal of initiative for a squaw, for she plunged straight into the subject which most nearly concerned Casey, and she was frank to the point of appalling him with her bluntness. Casey is a rather case-hardened bachelor, but I suspect that Lucy Lily scared him from the beginning.

"Do you like me when I have pretty dress on?" she inquired, smoothing the red silk complacently over her knees.

Casey swears that he told her it didn't make a darn bit of difference to him what she wore. If that is the truth, Lucy Lily must have been very stupid or very persistent, for she went on blandly stating her plans and her dearest wish.

"That gold mine I am keeping for my husband," she announced. "It is a present for a wedding gift for my man. I shall not marry an Indian man. I am too pretty and I have a gold mine, and I will marry a white man. Indians don't know what money is good for. I want to live in a town and wear silk dresses all the time every day and ride in a red automobile and have lots of rings and go to shows. Have you got lots of money?"

I don't know what Casey told her. He says he swore he hadn't a nickel to his name.

"I think you have got lots of money. I think perhaps you are rich. I don't see white men walk in the desert with silk shirts and have lots of jam and pickles if they are not rich. I think you want that gold mine awful bad. You gave Jim lots of jam so he would tell you. White men want lots of more money when they have got lots of money. It is like that in shows. If a man is poor he don't care. If a man is rich he is hunting all the time for more money and killing people. So I think you are like them rich mans in shows."

Casey told her again that he was poor; but she couldn't have believed him,— not in the face of all the silk and sweets he had displayed.

"I am awful glad Jim is dead. Now you have gave me the things. We will go to Tonopah and you will buy a red automobile and we will ride in it. And you will buy me lots of silk and rings. I shall be a lady like a princess in a show."

"Your mother has got something to say about that gold mine," Casey blurted desperately. "It's hers by rights. She'd have to go fifty-fifty on it. She's got it coming, and I never cheated anybody yet. I ain't going to commence on an old squaw."

"She is a big fool. What you think Hahnaga want of money? The agent he gives her blankets and tea and flour. If you give Hahnaga silk, I will be awful mad. She is old. She will die pretty quick."

"Well," said Casey, "I dunno as any of us has got any cinch on living. And if there's a gold mine in the family, she sure has got to have an even break. What about old Jim? Buried him yet?"

"He is in the tepee. I think Hahnaga will dig a grave. I don't care. I will go with you, and we will find the gold mine. Then you will buy me—"

"I'll buy you nothin'!" Casey's tone was emphatic.

Lucy Lily looked at him steadily. "Before we go for the gold mine we will go to Tonopah and get marriage, and you will give me a gold ring on my finger. Then I will show you where is gold so much you will have money to buy the world full of things." She smiled at him, showing her gold tooth. "I like you for my man," she said. "I am awful pretty. I have lots of fellows. I could marry lots of other white mans, but I will marry you."

"Like hell you will!" snorted Casey, and began to wipe out his frying pan and empty his coffeepot and make other preparations for instant packing. "Like hell you'll marry me! Think I'd marry a squaw—?"

"Then I will not tell you where is the gold! Then I hate you and I will fix you good! You want that gold mine awful bad. You will have to marry me before I tell you."

Casey straightened and looked at her, his frying pan in one hand, his coffeepot in the other. "Say,

I never asked you about the darn mine, did I? I done my talkin' to Injun Jim. It's you that butted in here on this deal. Seein' he's dead, I'll talk to his squaw and make a deal with her, mebby." He looked her over measuringly. " Princess — hunh! I'll tell yuh in plain American what you are, if yuh don't git outa here. I may want a gold mine, all right, but I sure don't want it that bad. Git when I tell yuh to git!"

A squaw with no education would have got forthwith. But Lucy Lily had learned to be like white ladies,— or so she said. She screamed at him in English, in Piute, and chose words in each that no princess should employ to express her emotions. Her loud denunciations followed Casey to the tepee, where he stopped and offered his services to Hahnaga as undertaker.

She accepted stolidly and together they buried Injun Jim, using his best blanket and not much ceremony. Casey did not know the Piute customs well enough to follow them, and his version of the white man's funeral service was simple in the extreme. Hahnaga, however, brought two bottles of pickles and one jar of preserves which had outlasted Injun Jim's appetite, and put them in the grave with him, together with his knife and an old rifle and his pipe.

To dig a grave and afterwards heap the dirt symmetrically over a discarded body takes a little time, no matter how cursory is the proceeding. Casey ceased to hear Lucy Lily's raucous voice and so thought that she had settled down. He misjudged

CASEY RYAN 179

the red princess. He discovered that when he went back to where William had stood.

He no longer stood there. He was gone, pack and all, and once more Casey stood equipped for desert journeying with shirt, overalls, shoes and socks, and his old Stetson, and with half a plug of tobacco, a pipe and a few matches in his pocket. On the bush where William had been tied a piece of paper was impaled and fluttered in the wind. Casey jerked it off and read the even, carefully formed script,— and swore.

"*Dear Sir:* I am going to Tonopah. If you try to come I will tell the sherf to coming and see Jim and put you in jail. I will tell the judge you killed him and the sherf will put you in jail and hung you. Those are fine shirts. I will wear them silk. As ever your friend,

      Yours truly,
      Lucy Lily."

Casey sat down on a rock to think it over. The squaw was moving about within the hut, collecting the pitifully few belongings which Lucy Lily had disdained to steal. An Indian does not like to stay where one has died.

Casey could overtake Lucy Lily, if he walked fast and did not stop when dark fell, but he did not want to overtake her. He was not alarmed at her threat of the sheriff, but he did not want to see her again or hear her or think of her.

So Casey tore up the note and went and begged a little food from Hahnaga; then he broached the subject of the gold mine. The squaw listened, looking at him with dull black eyes and a face like a stamped-leather portrait of an Indian. She shook her head and pointed down the gulch.

"No find gol', bad girl. I think killum my mans. I dunno. No fin' gol'— Jim he no tellum. No tellum me, no tellum Lucy, no tellum nobody. I think, all time Jim hide." She made a gesture as of one covering something with dirt. "Lucy all time try for fin' gol'. Jim he no likeum. Lucy my sister girl. Bad. No good. All time heap mean. All time tellum heap big lie so Indian no likeum. One time take monee, go 'way off. School for write. Come back for fin' gol', make Jim tellum. Jim sick long time. Jim no tellum. Jim all time mad for Lucy. Las' night — talk mean — mebby fight — Jim he die quick. Lucy say killum me, I tell.

"Now me go my brother. Walk two day. Give you grub — no got many grub. You takeum gol' you fin'. Me no care. No want. You don' give Lucy. Lucy bad girl all time. No fin' gol'— Jim he no tellum. I dunno."

That left Casey exactly where he had been before he found Injun Jim. There was no getting around it; the squaw repeated her statements twice, which Casey thought was probably more talking that she had done before in the course of six months. She impressed Casey as being truthful. She really did not know any more about Injun Jim's mine than did Casey. Or perhaps a little more, because she knew, poor thing, just how drunk Jim could get on the whisky they gave him for the gold. He used to beat her terribly when he came to camp drunk. Casey learned that much, though it didn't help him any.

Hahnaga did not seem to think that anything need be done about the manner of Jim's death. She said he was heap sick and would die anyway, or words — not many — to that effect. Casey decided to go on and mind his own business. He did not see why, he said, the county of Nye should be let in for a lot of expense on Injun Jim's account, even if Jim had been killed. And as for punishing Lucy Lily, he was perfectly willing that it should be done, only he did not want to do it. I have always believed that Casey was afraid she might possibly marry him in spite of himself if she were in his immediate neighborhood long enough.

They made themselves each a small pack of food and what was more vital, water, and went their different ways. Hahnaga struck off to the west, to her brother at the end of Forty-Mile Canyon. At least, that was where she said her brother mostly camped. Casey retraced his steps for the second time to the camp of the tenderfeet. Loco Canyon, Casey calls the place, claiming it by right of discovery.

Now I don't see, and possibly you won't see, either, what the devil's lantern had to do with Casey's bad luck. Casey maintains rather stubbornly that it had a great deal to do with it. First, he says, it got him all off the trail following it, and was almost the death of him and William. Next, he declares that it drove him to Lucy Lily and had fully intended that he should be tied up to her. Then he suspects that it had something to do with Injun Jim's dying just when he did, and he has another count or two against the lantern and will tell you them, and back them with much argument, if you nag him into it.

It taught him things, he says. And once, after we had talked the matter over and had fallen into silence, he broke out with a sentence I have never forgotten, nor the tone in which he said it, nor the way he glared into the fire, his pipe in his hand where he always had it when he was extremely in earnest.

"The three darndest, orneriest, damndest things on earth," said Casey, as if he were intoning a text, "is a Ford, or a goat, or an Injun. You can ask anybody yuh like if that ain't so."

CHAPTER XVIII

Casey was restless, and his restlessness manifested itself in a most unusual pessimism. Twice he picked up "float" that showed the clean indigo stain of silver bromyrite in spots the size of a split pea, and cast the piece from him as if it were so much barren limestone, without ever investigating to see where it had come from. Little as I know about mineral, I am sure that one piece at least was rich; high-grade, if ever I saw any. But Casey merely grunted when I spoke to him about it.

"Maybe it is. A coupla hundred ounces, say. What's that, even with silver at a dollar an ounce? It ain't good enough for Casey, and what I'm wastin' my time for, wearing the heels off'n my shoes prospectin' Starvation, is somethin' I can't tell yuh." He looked at me with his pale-blue, unwinking stare for a minute.

"Er — I can — and I guess the quicker it's out the better I'll feel."

He took out his familiar plug of tobacco, always nibbled around the edges, always half the size of his four fingers. I never saw Casey with a fresh plug in his pocket, and I never saw him down to one chew; it is one of the little mysteries in his life that I never quite solved.

"I been thinkin' about that devil's lantern we

seen the other night," he said, when he had returned to his pocket the plug with a corner gone. "They's something funny about that — the way it went over there and stood on the Tippipahs again. I ain't sooperstitious. But I can't git things outa my head. I want to go hunt fer that mine of Injun Jim's. This here is just foolin' around — huntin' silver. I want to see where that free gold comes from that he used to peddle. It's mine — by rights. He was goin' to tell me where it was, you recollect, and he woulda if I hadn't overfed him on jam — or if that damn squaw hadn't took a notion for marryin'. I let her stampede me — and that's where I was wrong. I shoulda stayed."

I was foolish enough to argue with him. I had talked with others about the mine of Injun Jim, and one man (who owned cattle and called mines a gamble) told me that he doubted the whole story. A prospectors' bubble, he called it. Free gold, he insisted, did not belong in this particular formation; it ran in porphyry, he said,— and then he ran into mineralogy too technical for me now. I repeated his statement, however, and saw Casey grin tolerantly.

"Gold is where yuh find it," he retorted, and spat after a hurrying lizard. "They said gold couldn't be found in that formation around Goldfield. But they found it, didn't they?"

Casey looked at me steadily for a minute and then came out with what was really in his mind. "You stake me to grub and a couple of burros an' let me go hunt the Injun Jim, and I'll locate yuh in on it when I find it. And if I don't find it, I'll pay yuh back for the outfit. And, anyway, you're makin' money off'n my bad luck right along, ain't yuh? Wasn't it me you was writin' up, these last few days?"

"I was — er — reconsidering that devil's lantern yarn you told me, Casey. But the thing doesn't work out right. It sounds unfinished, as you told it. I don't know that I can do anything with it, after all." I was truthful with him; you all remember that I was dissatisfied with the way Casey ended it. Just walking back across the desert and quitting the search,— it lacked, somehow, the dramatic climax. I could have built one, of course. But I wanted to test out my theory that a man like Casey will live a complete drama if he is left alone. Casey is absolutely natural; he goes out after life without waiting for it to come to him, and he will forget all about his own interests to help a stranger, — and above all, he builds his castles hopefully as a child and seeks always to make them substantial structures afterwards. If any man can prove my theory, that man is Casey Ryan. So I led him along to say what dream held him now.

"Unfinished? Sure it's unfinished! I quit, didn't I tell yuh? It ain't goin' to be finished till I git out and find that mine. I been studyin' things over. I never seen one of them lights till I started out to find Injun Jim's mine. If I'd a-gone along with no bad luck, I wouldn't never a-found that tenderfoot camp, would I? It was keepin' the light at my back done that — and William not likin' the look of it, either. And you gotta admit it was the light mostly that scared them young dudes off and left me the things. And if you'd of saw Injun Jim, you'd of known same as I that it was the jam and the silk shirts that loosened him up. Nothin' in my own pack coulda won him over,—"

"It's all right that far," I cut in. "But then he died, and you were set afoot and all but married by as venomous a creature as I ever heard of, and the thing stops right there, Casey, where it shouldn't."

"And that's what I'm kickin' about! Casey Ryan ain't the man to let it stop there. I been thinkin' it over sence that devil's lantern showed up again, and went and set over there on Tippipah. Mebby I misjudged the dog-gone thing. Mebby it's settin' somewheres around that gold mine. Funny it never showed up no other time and no other place. I been travelin' the desert off'n on all my life, and I never seen anything like it before. And I can tell yuh this much: I been wanting that mine too darn long to give up now. If you don't feel like stakin' me for the trip, I'll go back to Lund and have a talk with Bill. Bill's a good old scout and he'll stake me to an outfit, anyway."

That was merely Casey's inborn optimism speaking. Bill *was* a good old scout, all right, but if he would grubstake Casey to go hunting the Injun Jim mine, then Bill had changed considerably.

The upshot of it was that we left Starvation the next morning, headed for town. And two days after that I had pulled myself out of bed at daybreak to walk down to his camp under the mesquite grove just outside of town. I drank a cup of coffee with him and wished him luck. Casey did not talk much. His mind was all taken up with the details of his starting,— whether to trust his water cans on the brown burro or the gray, and whether he had taken enough "cold" shoes along for the mule. And he set down his cup of coffee to go rummaging in a kyack just to make sure that he had the hoof rasp and shoeing hammer safe.

He was packed and moving up the little hill out of the grove before the sun had more than painted a cloud or two in the east. A dreamer once more gone to find the end of his particular rainbow, I told myself, as I watched him out of sight. I must admit that I hoped, down deep in the heart of me, that Casey would fall into some other unheard-of experience such as had been his portion in the past. I felt much more certain that he would get into some scrape than I did that he would find the Injun Jim, and I was grinning inside when I went back to town; though there was a bit of envy in the smile,— one must always envy the man who keeps his dreams through all the years and banks on them to the end. For myself, I hadn't chased a rainbow for thirty years, and I could not call myself the better for it, either.

In September the lower desert does not seem to realize that summer is going. The wind blows a little harder, perhaps, and frequently a little hotter; the nights are not quite so sweltering, and the very sheets on one's bed do not feel so freshly baked.

But up on the higher mesas there is a heady quality to the wind that blows fresh in your face. There is an Indian-summery haze like a thin veil over the farthest mountain ranges. Summer is with you yet; but somehow you feel that winter is coming.

In a country all gray and dull yellow and brown, you find strange, beautiful tints no artist has yet prisoned with his paints. You dream in spite of yourself, and walk through a world no more than half real, a world peopled with your thoughts.

Casey did, when the burros left him in peace long enough. They were misleading, pot-bellied animals that Casey hazed before him toward the Tippipahs. They never showed more than slits of eyes beneath their drooping lids, yet they never missed seeing whatever there was to see, and taking advantage of every absent-minded moment when Casey was thinking of the Injun Jim, perhaps. They were fast-walking burros when they were following a beaten trail and Casey was hard upon their heels, but when his attention wandered they showed a remarkable amount of energy in finding blind trails and following them into some impracticable wash where Casey wasted a good deal of time in extricating them. He said he never saw burros that hated so to turn around and go back into the road, and he never saw two burros get out of sight as quickly as they could when they thought he wasn't watching. They would choose different directions and hide from him separately,— but once was enough for Casey. He lost them both for an hour in the sand pits twelve miles out of town, and after that he tied them nose to tail and himself held a rope attached to the hindmost, and so made fair time with them, after all.

The mule, Casey said, was just plain damn mule, sloughed off from the army, blasé beyond words,— any words at Casey's command, at least. A lop-eared buckskin mule with a hanging lower lip and a chronic tail-switching, that shacked along hour after hour and saved Casey's legs and, more particularly, a bunion that had developed in the past year.

Casey knew the country better than he had known it on his first unprofitable trip into the Tippipahs. He avoided Furnace Lake, keeping well around the southern rim of it and making straight for Loco Canyon and the spring there while his water cans still had a pleasant slosh. There he rested his long-ears for a day, and disinterred certain tenderfoot luxuries which he had cached when he was there last time. And when he set out again he went straight on to the old stone hut where Injun Jim had camped. The tepee was gone, burned down according to Indian custom after a death, as he had expected. The herd of Indian ponies were nowhere in sight. Hahnaga's brother, he guessed, had driven them off long ago.

Casey had worked out a theory, bit by bit, and with characteristic optimism he had full faith that it would prove a fact later on. He wanted to start his search from the point where Injun Jim had started, and he had rather a plausible reason for doing so.

Injun Jim was an Indian of the old school, and the old school did a great deal of its talking by signs.

Casey had watched Jim with that pale, unwinking stare that misses nothing within range, and he had read the significance of Jim's unconscious gestures while he talked. It had been purely subconscious; Casey had expected the exact location of the mine in words, and perhaps with a crudely accurate map of Jim's making. But now he remembered Jim's words, certain motions made by the skinny hands, and from them he laid his course.

"He was layin' right here — facin' south," Casey told himself, squatting on his heels within the rock circle that marked the walls of the tepee. "He said, 'Got heap big gol' mine, me —' and he turned his hand that way." Casey squinted at the distant blue ridge that was an unnamed spur of the Tippipahs. "It's far enough so an old buck like him couldn't make it very well. Fifteen mile, anyway — mebby twenty or twenty-five. And from the sign talk he made whilst he was talkin', I'd guess it's nearer twenty than fifteen. There's that two-peak butte — looks like that would be about right for distance. And it's dead in line — them old bucks don't waggle their hands permiskus when they talk. Old Jim woulda laid on his hands if he'd knowed what they was tellin' me; but even an ornery old devil like him gits careless when they git old. Casey hits straight fer Two Peak."

That's the way he got his bearings; just remembering the unguarded motion of Injun Jim's grimy hand and adding thereto his superficial knowledge of the country and his own estimate of what an old fellow like Jim could call a long journey. With this and the unquestioning faith in his dream that was a part of him, Casey threw his favorite "packer's hitch" across the packed burros at dawn next morning, boarded his buckskin mule and set off hopefully across the barren valley, heading straight for the distant butte he called Two Peak.

CHAPTER XIX

I don't suppose Casey Ryan ever started out to do something for himself — something he considered important to his own personal welfare and happiness — without running straight into some other fellow's business and stopping to lend a hand. He says he can't remember being left alone at any time in his life to follow the beckoning finger of his own particular destiny.

Casey had made camp that night in one of several deep gulches that ridged the butte with two peaks. We had been lucky in our burro buying, and he had two of the fastest walking jacks in the country, so that he was able to give them a good long nooning and still reach the foot of the butte and make camp well before sundown. For the first time since he first heard of the Injun Jim gold mine, Casey felt that he was really "squared away" to the search. As he sat there blowing his unhurried breath upon a blue granite cup of coffee to cool it, his memory slanted back along the years when he had said that some day he would go and hunt for the Injun Jim mine that was so rich a ten-pound lard bucket full of the ore had been known to yield five hundred dollars' worth of gold. Well, it had been a long time since he first said that to himself, but here he was, and to-morrow he would begin his search with daylight, starting with this gulch he was in and working methodically over every foot of Two Peak.

He took two long, satisfying swallows of coffee and poised the cup and listened. After a minute had gone in that way, he finished the coffee in gulps and stood up, dangling the empty cup with a finger crooked in the handle. From somewhere not more than a long rifle-shot away, a Ford was coughing under full pressure of gas and with at least one dirty spark plug to give it a spasmodic stutter. While Casey stood there listening, the stutter slowed and stopped with one wheezy cough. That was all.

"They'll have to clean up her hootin'-annies before they git outa here," Casey observed shrewdly, having intimate and sometimes unpleasant knowledge of Fords and their peculiar ailments. "And I wonder what the sufferin' Chris'mas they're doin' here, anyway. If it's huntin' the Injun Jim they're after, the quicker they scrape the sut off them dingbats and git outa here, the healthier they'll ride. You ask anybody if Casey Ryan's liable to back up now he's on the ground and squared away!"

He stood there uneasily for a minute or two longer, caught a whiff of his bacon scorching and stooped to its rescue. Then he fried a bannock hastily in the bacon grease, folded two slices of bacon within it and ate in a hurry, keeping an ear cocked for any further sounds from the concealed car.

He finished eating without having heard more and piled his dishes without washing them. I don't suppose he had used more than ten minutes at the longest in eating his supper. That was about the limit of Casey's inaction when he smelled a mystery or a scrap. This had the elements of both, and he started out forthwith to trail down the Ford, wiping crumbs from his mouth and getting out his plug of tobacco as he went.

In broken country sounds are deceptive as to direction, but Casey was lucky enough to walk straight toward the spot, which was over a hump in the gulch, a sort of backbone dividing it in two narrow branches there at its mouth. He had noticed when he rode toward it that it was ridged in the middle, and had chosen the left-hand branch for no reason at all except that it happened to be a little smoother traveling for his animals.

He topped the ridge and came full upon a camp below, almost within calling distance from where he first sighted it. There was a stone hut that could not possibly contain more than two small rooms, and there was a tent pitched not far away. There seemed to be a spring just beyond the cabin. Casey saw the silver gleam of water there, and a strip of green grass, and a juniper bush or two.

But these details were not important at the moment. What sent him down the hill in an uneven trot was a group of three that stood beside a car. From their voices, and the gestures that were being made, here was a quarrel building rapidly into a fight. To prove it the smallest person in the group suddenly whipped out a revolver and pointed it at the two. Casey saw the reddening sunlight strike upon the barrel with a brief shine, instantly quenched when the gun was thrust forward toward the other two whom it threatened.

"You get out of my camp and out of my sight just as fast as your legs can take you. This car belongs to me, and you're not going to touch it. You've got your wages — more than your wages, you great hulking shirks! A fine exhibition you're making of yourselves, I must say! You thought you could bluff me — that I'd stand meekly by and let you two bullies have your own way about it, did you? You even waited until you had gorged yourselves on food you've never earned, before you started your highwaymen performance. You made sure of one more good meal, you — you *hogs*. Now go, before I empty this gun into the two of you!"

Casey stopped, puffing a little, I suppose. He is not so young as when they called him the Fightin' Stagedriver, and he had done his long day of travel. The three did not know that he was there, they were so busy with their quarrel. The woman's voice was sharp with contempt, but it was not loud and there was not a tremble in any tone of it. The gun she held was steady in her hand, but one man snarled at her and one man laughed. It was the kind of laugh a woman would hate to hear from a man she was defying.

"Aw, puddown the popgun! Nobody's scared of it — er you. It ain't loaded, and if it was loaded you couldn't hit nothin'. No need to be scared 'long's a woman's pointing a gun *at* yuh. Crank 'er up, agin, Ole. Don't worry none about *her*. She can't stop nothin', not even her jawin'. Go awn, start the damn Lizzie an' let's go."

Ole bent to the cranking, then complained that the switch must be off. His companion growled that it was nothing of the kind and kept his narrowed gaze fixed upon the woman.

She spied Casey standing there, a few rods beyond the car. The gun dropped in her hand so that its aim was no longer direct. The man who faced her jumped and caught her wrist, and the gun went off, the bullet singing ten feet above Casey's head.

A little girl with flaxen curls and patched overalls on screamed and rushed up to the man, gripping him furiously around the legs just above the knees and trying her little best to shake him. "You leave my mamma alone!" she cried shrilly.

Casey took a hand then,— a hand with a rock in it, I must explain. He managed to kick Ole harshly in the ribs, sending him doubled sidewise and yelping, as he passed him. He laid the other man out senseless with the rock which landed precisely on the back of the head just under his hat.

The woman — Casey had mistaken her for a man at first, because she wore bib overalls and had her hair bobbed and a man's hat on — dropped the gun and held her wrist that showed angry red finger prints. She smiled at Casey exactly as if nothing much had happened.

"Thank you very much indeed. I was beginning to wonder how I was going to manage the situation. It was growing rather awkward, because

I should have been compelled to shoot them both, I expect, before I was through. And I dreaded a mess. Wounded, I should have had them on my hands to take care of — their great hulks! — and dead I should have had to bury them, and I detest digging in this rocky soil. You really did me a very great —"

Her eyes ranged to something behind Casey and widened at what they saw. Casey whirled about, ducked a hurtling monkey wrench and rushed Ole, who was getting up awkwardly, his eyes malevolent. He made a very thorough job of thrashing Ole, and finished by knocking him belly down over the unhooded engine of the Ford.

"I hope Jawn doesn't suffer from that," the little woman commented whimsically. "Babe, run and get that rope over there and take it to the gentleman so he can tie Ole's hands together. Then he can't be naughty any more. Hurry, Baby Girl."

Baby Girl hurried, her curls whipping around her face as she ran. She brought a coil of cotton clothesline to Casey, looking up at him with wide, measuring eyes of a tawny shade like sunlight shining through thin brown silk. "I wish you'd give Joe a beating too," she said with grave earnestness. "He's a badder man than Ole. He hurt my mamma. Will you give Joe a beating and tie his naughty hands jus' like that when he wakes up?" She lifted her plump little body on her scuffed toes, her brown, dimpled fingers clutching the radiator to hold her steady while she watched Casey tie Ole's naughty hands behind his back.

"Now will you tie Joe's naughty hands jus' like that? *Don't* use up all the rope! My mamma hasn't got any more rope, and you have to tie —"

"Babe! Come over here and don't bother the gentleman. Stand away over there so you can't hear the naughty words Ole is saying." The little woman smiled, but not much. Casey, glancing up from the last efficient knot, felt suddenly sorry that he had not first gagged Ole. Casey had not thought of it before; mere cussing was natural to him as breathing, and he had scarcely been aware of the fact that Ole was speaking. Now he cuffed the Swede soundly and told him to shut up, and yanked him off the car.

"Joe is regaining consciousness. He'll be nasty to handle as a rabid coyote if you wait much longer. Just cut the rope. It's my clothesline, but we must not balk at trifles in a crisis like this." The little woman had recovered her gun and was holding it ready for Joe in case the predicted rabidness became manifest.

Casey tied Joe very thoroughly while consciousness was slowly returning. The situation ceased to be menacing; it became safe and puzzling and even a bit mysterious. Casey reached for his plug, remembered his manners and took away his hand. Robbed of his customary inspiration he stood undecided, scowling at the feebly blinking ruffian called Joe.

"It's very good of you not to ask what it's all about," said the little woman, taking off the man's hat and shaking back her hair like a schoolgirl. "I have some mining claims here — four of them.

My husband left them to me, and since that's all he did leave I have been keeping up the assessment work every year. Last year I had enough money to buy Jawn." She nodded toward the Ford. " I outfitted and came out here with an old fellow I'd known for years, kept camp until he'd done the assessment work, and paid him off and that was all there was to it.

"This summer the old man is prospecting the New Jerusalem, I expect. He died in April. I hired these two scoundrels. I was foolish enough to pay half their wages in advance, because they told me a tale of owing money to a widow for board and wanting to pay her. I have," she observed, " a weakness for widows. And they have just pretended to be working the claims. I hurt my ankle so that I haven't been able to walk far for a month, and they took advantage of it and have been prospecting around on their own account, at my expense, while I religiously marked down their time and fed them. They have located four claims adjoining mine, and put up their monuments and done their location work in the past month, if you please, while I supposed they were working for me."

" D'they locate you in on 'em?"

" Locate me — in? You mean, as a partner? They emphatically did not! I went up to the claims to-day, saw that they had not done a thing since the last time I was there; they had even taken away my tools. So we tracked them, Baby and I, and found their location monuments just over the hill, and saw where they had been working. So to-night I asked them about it, and they were very defiant and very cool and decided that they were through out here and would go to town. They were *borrowing* Jawn — so they said. I was objecting, naturally. I was quite against being left alone out here, afoot, with Babe on my hands. It will soon be coming on cold," she said. " I'd have been in a fine predicament, with supplies for only about a month longer. And I must get the assessment work done, too, you know."

" D'you want 'em to stay and finish your work? " Casey reached out with his foot and pushed Joe down upon his back again.

The little woman looked down at Joe and across at Ole by the car. " No, thank you. I should undoubtedly put strychnine in their coffee if they stayed, I should hate the sight of them so. I have some that I brought for the pack rats. No, I don't want them —"

She had sounded very cool and calm, and she had impressed Casey as being quite as fearless as himself. But now he caught a trembling in her voice, and he distinctly saw her lip quiver. He was so disturbed that he went over and slapped Ole again and told him to shut up, though Ole was not saying a word.

" Where's their bed-rolls? " Casey asked, when he turned toward her again. She pointed to the tent, and Casey went and dragged forth the packed belongings of the two. It was perfectly plain that they had deliberately planned their desertion, for everything was ready to load into the car.

Casey went staggering to the Ford, dumped the

canvas rolls in and yanked Ole up by the collar, propelling him into the tonneau. Then he came after Joe.

"If you can drive, you'll mebby feel better if yuh go along," he said to the woman. "I'm goin' to haul 'em far enough sos't they won't feel like walkin' back to bother yuh, and seein' you don't know me, mebby you better do the drivin'. Then you'll know I ain't figurin' on stealin' your car and makin' a getaway."

"I can drive, of course," she acquiesced. "Not that I'd be afraid to trust Jawn with you, but they're treacherous devils, those two, and they might manage somehow to make you trouble if you go alone. Jawn is a temperamental car, and he demands all of one's attention at times."

She walked over to the car, reached out in the gathering dusk and fingered the carburetor adjustment. "When they first revealed their plan of making away with Jawn," she drawled, "I came up like this and remonstrated. And while I did so I reached over and turned the screw and shut off the gas feed. Jawn balked with them, of course — but they never guessed why!"

The two in the tonneau muttered something in undertones while the little woman smiled at them contemptuously. Casey thought that was pretty smart — to stall the car so they couldn't get away with it — but he did not tell her so. There was something about the little woman which restrained him from talking freely and speaking his mind bluntly as was his habit.

He cranked the car, waited until she had the adjustment correct, and then went back and stood on the running board, holding with his left hand to a brace of the top and keeping his right free in case he should need it. The little woman helped the little girl into the front seat, slid her own small person behind the wheel and glanced round inquiringly, with a flattering recognition of his masculine right to command.

"Just head towards town and keep a-going till I say when," he told her, and she nodded and sent Jawn careening down over the rough tracks which Casey had missed by a quarter of a mile or less.

She could drive, Casey admitted, almost as recklessly as he could. He had all he wanted to do, hanging on without being snapped off at some of the sharp turns she made. The road wandered down the valley for ten miles, crept over a ridge, then dove headlong into another wide, shallow valley seamed with washes and deep cuts. The little woman never eased her pace except when there was imminent danger of turning Jawn bottomside up in a wash. So in a comparatively short time they were over two summits and facing the distant outline of Crazy Woman Hills. They had come, Casey judged, about twenty miles, and they had been away from camp less than an hour.

Casey leaned forward and spoke to the woman, and she stopped the car obediently. Casey pulled open the door and motioned, and the Swede came stumbling out, sullenly followed by Joe, who muttered thickly that he was sick and that the back of his head was caved in. Casey did not reply, but heaved their bedding out after them. With the little woman holding her gun at full aim, he untied the two and frugally stowed the rope away in the car.

"Now, you git," he ordered them sternly. "There's four of us camped just acrost the ridge from this lady's place, and we'll sure keep plenty of eyes out. If you got any ideas about taking the back trail, you better think agin, both of yuh. You'd never git within shootin' distance of this lady's camp. I'm Casey Ryan that's speakin' to yuh. You ask anybody about me. Git!"

Sourly they shouldered their bed-rolls and went limping down the trail, and when their forms were only blurs beyond the shine of the headlights, the little woman churned Jawn around somehow in the sand and drove back quite as recklessly as she had come. Casey, bouncing alone in the rear seat, did a great deal of thinking, but I don't believe he spoke once.

"Casey Ryan, I have never had much reason for feeling gratitude toward a man, but I am truly grateful to you. You are a man and a gentleman." The little woman had driven close to the stone cabin and had turned and rested her arm along the back of the front seat, half supporting the sleeping child while she looked full at Casey. She had left the engine running, probably for sake of the headlights, and her eyes shone dark and bright in the crisp starlight.

"'Tain't worth mentionin'," Casey protested awkwardly, and got out.

"I've been wondering if I could get a couple of you men to do the work on my claims," she went on. "I'm paying four dollars and board, and it would be a great nuisance to make the long trip to town and find a couple of men I would dare trust. In fact, it's going to be pretty hard for me to trust any one, after this experience. If you men can take the time from your own business—"

"I don't know about the rest," Casey hedged uncomfortably. "They was figurin' on doing something else. But I guess I could finish up the work for yuh, all right. How deep is your shaft?"

"It's a tunnel," she corrected. "My husband started four years ago to drift in to the contact. He'd gone fifty feet when he died. I don't know that I'll strike the body of ore when I do reach the contact, but it's the only hope. I'm working the four claims as a group, and the tunnel is now eighty feet. Those two brigands have wasted a month for me, or it would be a hundred. One man can manage, though of course it's slower and harder. I have powder enough, unless they stole it from me. They did about five feet all told, and tore down part of my wall, I discovered to-day, chasing a stringer of fairly rich ore, thinking, I suppose, that it would lead to a pocket. The old man I had last year found a pocket of high grade that netted me a thousand dollars."

Casey threw up his head. "Gold?" he asked.

"Mostly silver. I sent a truck out from town after the ore, shipped it by express and still made a thousand dollars clear. There wasn't quite a ton and a half of it, though. You'll come, then, and work for me? I wish you could persuade one of your partners to help. It's getting well into September already."

"I wouldn't depend on 'em," Casey demurred uncomfortably. "I can do it alone. And I'll board m'self, if you'd ruther. I've got grub enough. I guess I better be gittin' along back to camp — if you ain't afraid to stay alone. Them two couldn't git back much b'fore daylight, if they run all the way; and by that time I'll be up and on the lookout," and Casey swung off without waiting for an answer.

CHAPTER XX

Casey was out of his blankets long before daylight the next morning and sitting behind a bush on the ridge just back of the cabin, his rifle across his knees. He hoped that his mention of three other men would discourage those two from the attempt to revenge themselves, much as a lone woman would tempt them. But he was not going to take any risk whatever.

At sunrise he went back to his camp — which he had moved closer to the cabin, by the way, just barely keeping it out of sight — and cooked a hasty breakfast. When he returned the little woman was ready to show him her claims, and she seemed to have forgotten those two who had been so ignominiously hauled away and dropped like unwanted cats beside the road. She inquired again about Casey's partners, and Casey lied once more and said that they had gone on over the range, prospecting.

I don't know why he did not tell the little woman that he had lied to Ole and Joe and let it go at that. But he seemed to dread having her discover that he had lied at all, and so he kept on lying about those three imaginary men. Perhaps he had a chivalrous instinct that she would feel safer, more at ease, if she thought that others were somewhere near. At any rate he did not tell her that his only partners were two burros and a mule.

I don't know what the little woman's opinion of Casey was, except that in the first enthusiasm of her gratitude to him she had called him a man and a gentleman. She drove a bargain with him, as she supposed. She would pay him so much more per day if he preferred to board himself, and having named the amount, Casey waited two minutes, as if he were meditating upon the matter, and then replied that it suited him all right.

Casey did not think much of her claims, though he did not tell her so. In his opinion that tunnel should have been driven into the hill at a different point, where the indications of mineral were much stronger and the distance to the contact much less. A light, varying vein had been followed at an incline, and Casey, working alone, was obliged to wheel every pound of dirt up a rather steep grade to the dump outside. The rock was hard to work in, so that it took him a full half a day to put in four shots, and then he would be likely to find that they had "bootlegged." The tunnel also faced the south, from where the wind nearly always blew, so that the gas and smoke from his shots would hang in there sometimes for a full twenty-four hours, making it impossible for him to work.

The little woman seemed slightly surprised when Casey told her, at the end of the first week, to knock off three days on account of gas. She and the little girl came to his camp next day and brought Casey a loaf of light bread and interrupted him in the act of shaving. The little woman looked at the two burros and at the mule, measured the camp outfit with her keen gray eyes, looked at Casey who had nicked his chin, and became thoughtful.

After that she stopped calling him Mr. Ryan and addressed him as Casey Ryan instead, with a little teasing inflection in her voice. Once Casey happened to mention Lund, and when he saw her look of surprise he explained that he drove a stage out of Lund, for awhile.

"Oh! So you *are* that Casey Ryan!" she said. "I might have known it." She laughed to herself, but she did not say why, and Casey was afraid to ask. He could remember so many incidents in his past that he would not want the little woman to know about, and he was afraid that it might be one of them at which she was laughing.

She formed the habit of coming up to the tunnel every day, with Babe chattering along beside her, swinging herself on her mother's hand. At first she said whimsically that she had found it best to keep an eye on her miners, as if that explained her coming. But she always had something good to eat or drink. Once she brought a small bucket of hot chocolate, which Casey gulped down heroically and smacked his lips afterwards. Casey hated chocolate, too, so I think you may take it for granted that by then he was a goner.

He used to smoke his pipe and watch the little woman and Babe go "high-grading" along the tunnel wall. That was what she called it and pretended that she expected to find very rich ore concealed somewhere. It struck him one day, quite suddenly, that the Little Woman (I may as well begin to use capitals, because Casey always called her that in his mind, and the capitals were growing bigger every day) the Little Woman never seemed to notice his smoking, or to realize that it is a filthy habit and immoral and degrading, as that other woman had done.

He began to notice other things, too; that the Little Woman helped him a lot, on afternoons when help was most likely to be appreciated. She sometimes "put down a hole" all by herself, skinning a knuckle now and then with the lightest "single-jack" and saying *"darn!"* quite as a matter of course.

And once, when the rock was particularly hard, she happened along and volunteered to turn the drill while Casey used the "double-jack", which I suppose you know is the big hammer that requires two hands to pound the drill while another turns it slightly after each blow, so that the bitted end will chew its way into hard rock.

You aren't all of you miners, so I will explain further that to drill into rock with a double-jack and steel drill is not sport for greenhorns exactly. The drill-turner needs a lot of faith and a little nerve, because one blow of the double-jack may break a hand clasped just below the head of the drill. And the man with the double-jack needs a steady nerve, too, and some experience in swinging the big hammer true to the head of the drill,— unless he enjoys cracking another man's bones.

Casey Ryan prides himself upon being able to swing a double-jack as well as any man in the country. It is his boast that he never yet broke the skin on the hand of his drill-turner. So I shall have to let you take it for granted that the Little Woman's presence and help was more unnerving than a wildcat on Casey's back. For, while the first, second and third blows fell true on the drill, the fourth went wild. Casey owns that he was in a cold sweat for fear he might hit her. So he did. She was squatted on her heels, steadying one elbow on her knee. The double-jack struck her hand, glanced and landed another blow on her knee; one of those terribly painful blows that take your breath and make you see stars without crippling you permanently.

Casey doesn't like to talk about it, but once he growled that he did about every damn-fool thing he could with a double-jack, except brain her. The Little Woman gave one small scream and went over backward in a faint, and Casey was just about ready to go off and shoot himself.

He took her up in his arms and carried her down to the cabin before she came to. And when she did come to her senses, Babe immediately made matters worse. She was whimpering beside her mother, and when she saw that mamma had waked up, she shrilled consolingly: "It's going to be all well in a minute. Casey Ryan kissed it des like *that!* So now it'll get all well!"

If the Little Woman had wanted to tell Casey what she thought of him, she couldn't just then, for Casey was halfway to his own camp by the time she glanced around the room, looking for him.

Common humanity drove him back, of course.

CASEY RYAN

He couldn't let a woman and a child starve to death just because he was a damned idiot and had half-killed the woman. But if there had been another person within calling distance, the Little Woman would probably never have seen Casey Ryan again.

Necessity has a bland way of ignoring such things as conventions and the human emotions. Casey cooked supper for Babe and the Little Woman, and washed the dishes, and wrung out cloths from hot vinegar and salt so that the Little Woman could bathe her knee — she had to do it left-handed, at that — and unbuttoned Babe's clothes and helped her on with her pyjamas and let her kneel on his lap while she said her prayers. Because, as Babe painstakingly explained, she always kneeled on a lap so ants couldn't run over her toes and tickle her and make her laugh, which would make God think she was a bad, naughty girl.

Can you picture Casey Ryan rocking that child to sleep? I can't — yes, I can too, and there's something in the picture that holds back the laugh you think will come.

Before she gave her final wriggle and cheeped her last little cheep, Babe had to be carried over and held down where she could kiss mamma good night. Casey got rather white around the mouth, then. But he didn't say a word. Indeed, he had said mighty little since that fourth blow of the doublejack; just enough to get along intelligently, with what he had to do. He hadn't even told the Little Woman he was sorry.

So Babe was asleep and tucked in her bed, and

Casey turned down the light and asked perfunctorily if there was anything else he could do, and had started for the door. And then —

"Casey Ryan," called the Little Woman, with the teasing note in her voice. "Casey Ryan, come back here and listen to me. You are not going off like that to swear at yourself all night. Sit down in that chair and listen to me!"

Casey sat down, swallowing hard. All the Casey Ryan nonchalance was gone,— never had been with him, in fact, while he faced that Little Woman. Somehow she had struck him humble and dumb from the very beginning. I wish I knew how she did it; I'd like to try it sometime myself.

"Casey Ryan, it's hard for a woman to own herself in the wrong, especially to a man," she said, when he had begun to squirm and wonder what biting words she would say. "I've always thought that I had as good nerve as any one. I have, usually. But that double-jack scared the life out of me after the first blow, and I thought I wouldn't let on. I couldn't admit I was afraid. I was terribly ashamed. I knew you'd never miss, but I was scared, just the same. And like a darn fool I pushed the drill away from me just as you struck. It was coming down — you couldn't change it, man alive. You'd aimed true at the drill, and — the drill wasn't just there at the moment. Serves me right. But it's tough on you, old boy — having to do the cooking for three of us while I'm laid up!"

I'm sure I can't see how Casey Ryan ever got the

name of being a devil with the ladies. He certainly behaved like a yap then, if you get my meaning. He gave the Little Woman a quick, unwinking stare, looked away from her shamedly, reached for his plug of tobacco, took away his hand, swallowed twice, shuffled his feet and then grunted — I can use no other word for it:

"Aw, I guess I c'n stand it if you can!"

He made a motion then to rise up and go to his own camp where he would undoubtedly think of many tender, witty things that he would like to have spoken to the Little Woman. But she was watching him. She saw him move and stopped him with a question.

"Casey Ryan, tell me the truth about that tunnel. Do you think it's ever going to strike the ore body at all?"

Start Casey off on the subject of mining and you have him anchored and interested for an hour, at least. The Little Woman had brains, you must see that.

"Well, I don't want to discourage you, ma'am," Casey said reluctantly, the truth crowding against his teeth. "But I'd 'a' gone in under that iron capping, if I'd been doing it. The outcropping you followed in from the surface never has been in place, ma'am. It's what I'd call a wild stringer. It pinched out forty foot back of where we're diggin' now. That's just an iron stain we're following, and the pocket of high grade don't mean nothin'. You went in on the strength of indications —" He stopped there and chuckled to himself, in a way that

I'd come to know as the "indications" of a story,— which usually followed.

The Little Woman probably guessed. I suppose she was lonely, too, and the pain of her hurts made her want entertainment. "What are you laughing at, Casey Ryan?" she demanded. "If it's funny, tell *me*."

Casey blushed, though she couldn't have seen him in the dusky light of the cabin. "Aw, it ain't anything much," he protested bashfully. "I just happened to think about a little ol' Frenchman I knowed once, over in Cripple Creek, ma'am." He stopped.

"Well? Tell me about the little ol' Frenchman. It made you laugh, Casey Ryan, and it's about the first time I've seen you do that. Tell me."

"Well, it ain't nothin' very funny to tell about," Casey hedged like a bashful boy; which was mighty queer for Casey Ryan, I assure you. For if there was anything Casey liked better than a funny story, it was some one to listen while he told it. "You won't git the kick, mebby. It's knowin' the Frenchman makes it seem kinda funny when I think about it. He was a good little man and he kept a little hotel and was an awful good cook. And he wanted a gold mine worse than anybody I ever seen. He didn't know a da — nothin' at all about minin' ma'am, but every ol' soak of a prospector could git a meal off him by tellin' him about some wildcat bonanza or other. He'd forgit to charge 'em, he'd be so busy listenin'.

"Well, there was two ol' soaks that got around him to grubstake 'em. They worked it all one year.

CASEY RYAN 215

They'd git a burro load of grub and go out somewheres and peck around till it was all et up, and then they'd come back an' tell Frenchy some wild tale about runnin' acrost what looked like the richest prospect in the country. They'd go on about havin' all the indications of a big body uh rich ore. He'd soak it in, an' they'd hang around town — one had a sore foot one time, I remember, that lasted 'em a month of good board at Frenchy's hotel before he drove 'em out agin to his mine, as he called it.

"They worked that scheme on him for a long time — and it was the only da — scheme they wasn't too lazy to work. They'd git money to buy powder an' fuse an' caps, ma'am, an' blow it on booze, y'see. An' they'd hang in town, boardin' off Frenchy, jest as long as they c'ld think of an excuse fer stayin'.

"So somebody tipped Frenchy off that he was bein' worked for grub an' booze money, an' Frenchy done a lot uh thinkin'. Next time them two come in, he was mighty nice to 'em. An' when he finally got 'em pried loose an' headed out, he appeared suddenly and says he's goin along to take a look at his mine. They couldn't do nothin' but take him, uh course. So they led him out to an old location hole somebody else had dug, an' they showed him iron cappin' an' granite contact an' so on —— just talkin' wild, an' every few minutes comin' in with the 'strong indications of a rich ore body.' That was their trump suit, y'see, ma'am.

"Frenchy listened, an' his eyes commenced to

snap, but he never said nothin' for awhile. Then all at once he pulled one uh these ol'-style revolvers an' points it at 'em, an' yells: '*Indicaziones! Indicaziones!* T'ell weez your *indicaziones!* Now you show me zee me-*tall!*'" Casey stopped, reached for his plug and remembered that he mustn't. The Little Woman laughed. She didn't seem to need the tapering off of the story, as most women demand.

"And so you think I have plenty of *indicaziones*, but mighty little chance of getting the me-*tall*," she pointed the moral. "Well, then tell me what to do."

It was in the telling, I think, that Casey for the first time forgot to be shy and became his real, Casey Ryan best. The Little Woman saw at once, when he pointed it out to her, that she ought to drift and cut under the iron capping instead of tunneling away from it as they had been doing.

But she was not altogether engrossed in that tunnel. I think her prospecting into the soul of Casey Ryan interested her much more; and being a woman she followed the small outcropping of his Irish humor and opened up a distinct vein of it before the evening was over. Just to convince you, she led him on until Casey told her all about feeding his Ford syrup instead of oil, and all about how it ran over him a few times on the dry lake,—Casey was secretly made happy because she saw at once how easily that could happen, and never once doubted that he was sober! He told her about the goats in Patmos and made her laugh so hard that Babe woke

CASEY RYAN

and whimpered a little, and insisted that Casey take her up and rock her again in the old homemade chair with crooked juniper branches hewn for rockers.

With Babe in his arms he told her, too, about his coming out to hunt the Injun Jim mine. He must have felt pretty well acquainted, by then, because he regaled her with a painstaking, Caseyish description of Lucy Lily and her educated wardrobe, and — because she was a murderous kind of squaw and entitled to no particular chivalry — even repeated her manner of proposing to a white man, and her avowed reason and all. That was going pretty far, I think, for one evening, but we must keep in mind the fact that Casey and the Little Woman had met almost a month before this, and that Casey had merely thrown wide open the little door to his real self.

At any rate it was after ten o'clock by Casey's Ingersoll when he tucked Babe into her little bed, brought a jelly glass of cold water for the Little Woman to drink in the night, and started for the door.

There he stopped for a minute, debated with his shyness and turned back.

"You mebby moved that steel at the wrong time," he said abruptly, "I guess you musta, the way it happened. But I was so scared I'd hit yuh, my teeth was playin' the dance to *La Paloma*. I was in a cold sweat. I never did hit a man with a doublejack in my life, and I guess I've put down ten miles uh holes, ma'am, if you placed 'em end to end. I always made it my brag I never scraped a knuckle at that game. But — them little hands of yours on the drill — I was shakin' all over for fear I might — hurt yuh. I — I never hated anything so bad in my life — I'd ruther kill a dozen men than hurt you —"

"Man alive," the Little Woman exclaimed softly from her dusky corner, "you'd never have hurt me in the world, if I'd had the nerve to trust you." And she added softly, "I'll trust you, from now on, Casey Ryan. Always."

I think Casey was an awful fool to walk out and never let her know that he heard that "Always."

CHAPTER XXI

"Casey Ryan," the Little Woman began with her usual abruptness one evening, when she was able to walk as far as the mine and back without feeling the effect of the exercise, but was still nursing a bandaged right hand; "Casey Ryan, tell me again just what old Injun Jim looked like."

Casey laughed and shifted Babe to a more secure perch on his shoulder, and drew his head to one side in an effort to slacken Babe's terrific pull on his hair. "Him? Mean an' ornery as the meanest thing you can think of. Sour as a dough can you've went off an' left for a coupla weeks in July."

"Oh, yes; very explicit, I admit. But just what did he look like? Height, weight, age and chief characteristics. I have," she explained, "a very good reason for wanting a description of him."

"What yuh want a description of him for? He's good an' dead now." You see, Casey had reached the point of intimacy where he could argue with the Little Woman quite in his everyday Irish spirit of contention.

The Little Woman had spirit of her own, but she was surprisingly meek with Casey at times. "It struck me quite suddenly, to-day, that I may know where that gold mine is; or about where it is," she said, with a hidden excitement in her voice. "I've been thinking all day about it, and putting two and two together. I merely need a fair description now of Injun Jim, to feel tolerably certain that I do or do not know something about the location of that mine."

"How'd *you* come to know anything about it?" Casey stopped to move Babe to his other shoulder. He had put in a long hard day in the tunnel, and Babe was a husky youngster for four-and-a-half. Also she had developed a burr-like quality toward Casey, and she liked so well to be carried home from the mine that she would sit flat on the ground and rock her small body and weep until she was picked up and placed on Casey's shoulder. "Set still, now, Babe, or Casey'll have to put yuh down an' make yuh walk home. Le'go my ear! Yuh want Casey to go around lop-sided, with only one ear?"

"Yes!" assented Babe eagerly, kicking Casey in the stomach. "Give me your knife, Casey Wyan, so I can cut off one ear an' *make* you lop-sided!"

"An' you'd do it, too!" Casey exclaimed admiringly.

"Baby Girl, you interrupted mother when mother was speaking of something important. You make mother very sad."

Babe's mouth puckered, her eyelids puckered, and she give a small wail. "Now Baby's sad! You hurt — my — *feelin's* when you speak to me cross!" She shook her yellow curls into her eyes and wept against them.

There was no hope of grown-ups talking about anything so foolish as a gold mine when Babe was in that mood. So Casey cooked supper, washed the dishes and helped Babe into her pyjamas; then he let her kneel restively in his lap while she said her prayers, and told her a story while he rocked her to sleep — it was a funny, Caseyish story about a bear, but we haven't time for it now — before he attempted to ask the Little Woman again what she meant by her mysterious curiosity concerning Injun Jim. Then, when he had his pipe going and the stove filled with piñon wood, he turned to her with the question in his eyes.

The Little Woman laughed. " Now, if that terrible child will kindly consent to sleep for fifteen minutes, I'll tell you what I meant," she said. " It had slipped my mind altogether, and it was only to-day, when Babe was scratching out a snake's track — so the snake couldn't find the way back home, she said — that I chanced to remember. Just a small thing, you know, that may or may not mean something very large and important — like a gold mine, for instance."

" I don't have to go to work 'til sunup," Casey hinted broadly, " and I've set up many a night when I wasn't havin' half as much fun as I git listenin' to you talk."

Again the Little Woman laughed. I think she had been rambling along just to bait Casey into something like that."

" Very well, then, I'll come to the point. Though it is such a luxury to talk, sometimes! For a woman, that is.

" Three years ago we had two burros to pack

water from your gulch, where there were too many snakes, to this gulch where there never seemed to be so many. We hadn't developed this spring then. One night something or other frightened the burros and they disappeared, and I started out to find them, leaving Babe of course with her father at the tunnel.

"I trailed those burros along the mountain for about four miles, I should think. And by that time I was wishing I had taken a canteen with me, though when I started out from camp I hated the thought of being burdened with the weight of it. I thought I could find water in some of the gulches, however, so I climbed a certain ridge and sat down to rest and examine the canyon beneath with that old telescope Babe plays with. It has been dropped so many times it's worthless now, but three years ago you could see a lizard run across a rock a mile away. Don't you believe that?" she stopped to demand sternly.

"Say! You couldn't tell me nothin' I wouldn't believe!" Casey retorted, fussing with his pipe to hide the grin on his face.

"This is the truth, as it happens. I merely speak of the lizard to convince you that a man's features would show very distinctly in the telescope. And please observe, Casey Ryan, that I am very serious at the moment. This may be important to you, remember.

"I was sitting among a heap of boulders that capped the ridge, and it happened that I was pretty well concealed from view because I was keeping in the shade of a huge rock and had crouched down so that I could steady the telescope across a flat rock in front of me. So I was not discovered by a man down in the canyon whom I picked up with the telescope while I was searching the canyon side for a spring.

"The man was suddenly revealed to me as he parted the branches of a large greasewood and peered out. I think it was the stealthiness of his manner that impressed me most. He looked up and down and across, but he did not see me. After a short wait, while he seemed to be listening, he crept out from behind the bush, turned and lifted forward a bag which hadn't much in it, yet appeared quite heavy. He went down into the canyon, picking his way carefully and stepping on rocks, mostly. But in one place where he must cross a wash of deep sand, he went backward and with a dead branch he had picked up among the rocks he scratched out each track as he made it. Babe reminded me of that to-day when she scratched out the snake's track in the sand up by the mine."

Casey was leaning toward her, listening avidly, his pipe going cold in his hand. "Was he—?"

"He was an Indian, and very old, and he walked with that bent, tottery walk of old age. He had one eye and—"

"Injun Jim, that was — couldn't be anybody else!" Casey knocked his pipe against the front of the little cookstove, emptying the half-burned tobacco into the hearth. The Little Woman probably wondered why he seemed so unexcited, but she did not know all of Casey's traits. He put away his pipe and almost immediately reached for his plug of tobacco, taking a chew without remembering where he was. "If you feel able to ride," he said, "I'll ketch up the mule in the morning, and we'll go over there."

"So your heart is really set on finding it, after all. I've been wondering about that. You haven't seemed to be thinking much about it, lately."

"A feller can prospect," Casey declared, "when he can't do nothin' else." And he added rather convincingly, "Good jobs is scarce, out this way. I'd be a fool to pass up this one, when I'd have the hull winter left fer prospectin'."

"And what about those partners of yours?"

"Oh, them?" Casey hesitated, tempted perhaps to tell the truth. "Oh, they've quit on me. They quit right away after I went to work. We — we had a kinda fuss, and they've went back to town." He stopped and added with a sigh of relief, "We can just as well count them out, fr'm now on — an' fergit about 'em."

"Oh," said the Little Woman, and smiled to herself. "Well, if you are anxious about that patch of brush in the canyon, we'll go and see what's behind it. To-morrow is Sunday, anyway."

"I'd a made up the time, if it wasn't," Casey assured her with dignity. "I've been waitin' a good many years for a look at that Injun Jim gold."

"And it's just possible that I have been almost within reach of it for the past four years and didn't know it! Well, I always have believed that Fate weaves our destinies for us; and a curious pattern is the weaving, sometimes! I'll go with you, Casey Ryan, and I hope, for your sake, that Indian Jim's mine is behind that clump of bushes. And I hope," she added, with a little laugh whose meaning was not clear to Casey, " I hope you get a million dollars out of it! I should like to point to Casey Ryan, the mining millionaire and say, ' That plutocratic gentleman over there once knocked me down with a hammer, and washed my dishes for two weeks, and really, my dears, you should taste his sour-dough biscuits!' "

Casey went away to his camp and lay awake a long time, not thinking about the Injun Jim mine, if you please, but wondering what he had done to make the Little Woman give him hell about his biscuits. Good Lord! Did she still blame him for hitting her with that double-jack? — when he knew and she knew that she had made him do it! — and if she didn't like his sour-dough biscuits, why in thunder had she kept telling him she did?

He tucked the incident away in the back of his mind, meaning to watch her and find out just what she did mean, anyway. Her opinion of him had become vital to Casey; more vital than the Injun Jim mine, even.

He saddled the buckskin mule next morning and after breakfast the three set out, with a lunch and two canteens of water. The Little Woman was in a very good humor and kept Casey " jumpin' sideways," as he afterwards confessed to me, wondering just what she meant or whether she meant nothing at all by her remarks concerning his future wealth and dignity and how he would forget old friends.

She even pretended she had forgotten the place, and was not at all sure that this was the right canyon, when they came to it. She studied landmarks and then said they were all wrong and that the place was marked in her mind by something entirely different and not what she first named. She deviled Casey all she could, and led him straight to the spot and suggested that they eat their lunch there, within twenty feet of the bushes from which she had seen the Indian creep with the sack on his back.

She underrated Casey's knowledge of minerals; or perhaps she wanted to test it,— you never can tell what a woman really has in the back of her mind. Casey sat there eating a sour-dough biscuit of his own making, and staring at the steep wall of the canyon because he was afraid to stare at the Little Woman, and so his uncannily keen eye saw a bit of rock no larger than Babe's fist. It lay just under that particular clump of bushes, in the shade. And in the shade he saw a yellow gleam on the rock.

He looked at the Little Woman then and grinned, but he didn't say anything until he had taken the coffeepot off the fire, and had filled her cup.

"This ain't a bad canyon to prospect in. You can brush up your memory whilst I take a look around. Mebby I can find Jim's mine myself," he said impudently. Then he got up and went poking here and there with his prospector's pick, and finally worked up to the brush and disappeared behind it.

In five minutes or less he came back to her with a little nugget the size of Babe's thumb.

"If yuh want to see something pretty, come on up where I got this here," he told her. "I'll show yuh what drives prospectors crazy. This ain't no free gold country, but there's a pile uh gold in a dirt bank I can show yuh. Mebby you forgot the place, and mebby yuh didn't. I've quit guessin' at what yuh really do mean an' what yuh don't mean. Anyway, this is where we headed for."

"Well, you really are a prospector, after all. I just wondered." The Little Woman did not seem in the least embarrassed. She just laughed and took Babe by the hand, and they went up beyond the clump of bushes to what lay hidden so cunningly behind it.

Cunning — that was the mood Nature must have been in when she planted free gold in that little wrinkle on the side of Two Peak, and set the bushes in the mouth of the draw, and piled an iron ledge across the top and spread barren mountainside all around it. In the hiding Injun Jim had done his share, too. He had pulled rubble down over the face of the bank of richness, and eyes less keen than Casey's would have passed it by without a second glance.

The Little Woman knelt and picked out half a dozen small nuggets and stood up, holding them out to Casey, her eyes shining. "Casey Ryan, here's the end of your rainbow! And you're luckier than most of us; you've got your pot o' gold."

Casey looked down at her oddly. "It's mebby

the end of one," he said. " But they's another one, now, 't I can see plainer than this one. I dunno's I'll ever git to where that one points."

" A man's never satisfied," scoffed the Little Woman, turning the precious little yellow fragments over thoughtfully in her palm. " I should think this ought to be enough for you, man alive."

" Mebby it had. But it ain't." He looked at her, hesitating,— and I think the Little Woman waited and held her breath for what he might say next. But Casey was scarcely himself in her presence. He turned away without another glance at the nuggets.

" You'n the kid can gopher around there whilst I go step off the lines of a claim an' put up the location notice," he said, and left her standing there with the gold in her palm.

That night it was the Little Woman who planned great things for Casey, and it was Casey who smoked and said little about it. But once he shook his head when she described the gilded future she saw for him.

" Money in great gobs like that ain't much use to me," he demurred. " Once I blew into Lund, over here, with twenty-five thousand dollars in my pocket that I got outa silver claims. All I ever saved outa that chunk was two pairs of socks. No need of you makin' plans on my being a millionaire. It ain't in me. I guess I'm nothin' but a rough-neck stagedriver an' prospector, clear into the middle of my bones. If I had the sense of a rabbit I never'd gone hellin' through life the way I've done. I'd

CASEY RYAN 229

amount to somethin' by now. As it is I ain't nothin' and I ain't nobody —"

"You're Casey Wyan! You make me sad when you say that!" Babe protested sleepily, lifting her head from his shoulder and spatting him reprovingly on the cheek. "You're my bes' friend and you've got a lots more sense than a wabbit!"

"And your rainbow, Casey Ryan?" the Little Woman asked softly. "What about this other, new rainbow?"

"It's there," said Casey gloomily. "It'll always be there — jest over the ridge ahead uh me. I c'n see it, plain enough, but I got more sense 'n to think I'll ever git m'hands on it."

"I'll go catch your wainbow, Casey Wyan. I'll run fas' as I can, an' I'll catch it for you!"

"Will yuh, Babe?" Casey bent his head until his lips touched her curls. And neither Casey nor the Little Woman spoke of it again.

CHAPTER XXII

Oddly enough, it was Lucy Lily who unconsciously brought Casey to his rainbow. Lucy Lily did not mean to do Casey any favor, I can assure you, but Fate just took her and used her for the moment, and Lucy Lily had nothing to say about it.

Don't think that a squaw who wants to live like a white princess will forget to go hunting a gold mine whose richness she had seen,— in a lard bucket, perhaps. Lucy Lily did not abandon her bait. She used it again, and a renegade white man snapped at it, worse luck. So they went hunting through the Tippipahs for the mine of Injun Jim. What excuses the squaw made for not being able to lead the man directly to the spot, I can't say, of course; but I suppose she invented plenty.

She did one clever thing, at least. In their wanderings she led the way into the old camp of Injun Jim. There had been no storm to dim the tracks Casey had made, and Lucy Lily, Indian that she was, knew that these were the tracks of Casey Ryan and guessed what was his errand there. So she and her white man trailed him across the valley to Two Peak.

They came first to the camp, and there the Little Woman met them, and by some canny intuition knew who they were and what they wanted,—

CASEY RYAN 231

thanks to Casey's garrulous mood when he told her of Lucy Lily. They said that they were hunting horses, and presently went on over the ridge; not following Casey's plain trail to the tunnel, but riding off at an angle so that they could come into the trail once they were hidden from the house.

Casey, as it happened, was not at the tunnel at all, but over at the gold mine, doing the location work. Doing it in the side hill a good two hundred feet away from the gold streak, too, I will add.

The Little Woman watched until the squaw and her man were out of sight, and then she took a small canteen and filled it, got her rifle, pocketed her automatic revolver, and tied Babe's sunbonnet firmly under Babe's double chin. She could not take the mule, because Casey had ridden him, so she walked, — and carried Babe most of the way on her back. She kept to the gulches until she was too far away to be seen in the sage, even when a squaw was squinting sharp-eyed after her.

She came, in the course of two hours or so, to the lip of the canyon, and who-whooed to Casey, mucking out after a shot he had put down in the location hole. Casey looked up, waved his hand and then came running. No whim would send the Little Woman on a four-mile walk with a heavy child like Babe to carry, and Casey was as white as he'll ever get when he met her halfway to the bottom of the canyon.

"Take Babe and let's get back to the claim," she panted. "I came to tell you that squaw is on your trail with a white man in tow, and it'll be a case of claim-jumping if they can see their way tolerably clear. He's a mate for the two you helped me haul out of camp, and I think, Casey Ryan, the squaw would kill you in a minute if she gets the chance."

Casey did rather a funny thing, considering how scared he was usually of the Little Woman. "You pack that kid all the way over here?" he grunted, and picked up the Little Woman and carried her, and left Babe to walk. Of course he helped Babe, holding her hand over the roughest spots, but it was the Little Woman whom he carried the rest of the way. And Babe, if you please, was quite calm about it and never once became "sad" so that she must sit down and cry.

"All the claim-jumpin' they'll do won't hurt nobody," Casey observed unexcitedly, when he had set the Little Woman down on a rock beside his location "cut" in the canyon's side. "She likely picked on a white man so's he could locate under the law, but this claim's located a'ready." He waved a hand toward the monument, a few rods up the canyon. "And Casey Ryan ain't spreadin' no rich gold vein wide open for every prowlin' desert rat to pack off all he kin stagger under. I'm callin' it the Devil's Lantern. You c'n call a mine any name yuh darn want to. And if it wasn't fer the Devil's Lantern, I wouldn't be here. That name won't mean nothin' to 'em. Let 'em come." His eyes turned toward the hidden richness and dwelt there, studying the tracks, big and little, that led up to it, and deciding that tracks do not necessarily mean a gold mine, and that it would be better to leave them as they were and not attempt to cover them.

"You just say it's your claim, if they come snoopin' around here. I'm supposed to be workin' for yuh," he said abruptly, giving her one of his quick, steady glances.

"They can go and read the location notice," the Little Woman pointed out. Casey did not make any reply to that, but picked up his shovel and went to work again, mucking out the dirt and broken rocks which the dynamite had loosened in the cut.

"She's a bird, ain't she?" he grinned over his shoulder, his mind reverting to Lucy Lily. "Did she have on her war paint?"

"She will have, when she sees you," the Little Woman retorted, watching the farther rim of the canyon. Then she remembered Babe and called to her. That youngster was always prospecting around on her own initiative, and she answered shrilly now from up the canyon. The Little Woman stood up, looking that way, never dreaming how wishfully Casey was watching her,— and how reverently.

"Baby Girl, you must *not* run off like that! Mother will be compelled to tie a rope on you."

"I was jes' getting — Casey Wyan's —'bacco. Poor Casey Wyan forgot — his 'bacco! He's my frien'. I have to give him his 'bacco," Babe defended herself, coming down from the location monument in small jumps and scrambles. Close to her importantly heaving chest she clutched a small, red tobacco can of the kind which smokers carelessly call "P.A." "Casey Wyan lost it up in the wocks," Babe explained, when her mother met her disapprovingly and caught her by the hand.

"Why, Babe! You've been naughty. This must be Casey Ryan's location notice. It must be left in the rocks, Baby Girl, so people will know that Casey Ryan owns this claim."

"It's his 'bacco!" Babe insisted stubbornly. "Casey Wyan needs his 'bacco."

The Little Woman knew that streak of stubbornness of old. There was just one way to deal with it, and that was to prove to Babe that she was mistaken. So she opened the red can and pulled out a folded paper, unfolded the paper and began to read it aloud. Not that Babe would understand it all, but to make it seem very convincing and important,— and I think partly to enjoy for herself the sense of Casey's potential wealth.

"'NOTICE OF LOCATION — QUARTZ,'" she read, and glanced over the paper at her listening small daughter. "'*To Whom it May Concern: Please take notice that: The name of this claim is the Devil's Lantern Quartz Mining Claim. Said Claim is situated in the — Unsurveyed — Mining District, County of Nye, State of Nevada. Located this twenty-fifth day of September, 19 —. This discovery is made and this notice is posted this twenty-fifth day of September, 19 —.*

2. That the undersigned locators are citizens of the United States or have declared their intention to become such, and have discovered mineral-bearing rock —!"

"What's mineral-bearing wock, mother?"

"That's the gold, Baby Girl. '— *in place thereon and do locate and claim same for mining purposes.*

3. That the number of linear feet in length along the course of the vein each way from the point of discovery whereon we have erected a monument —' That's the monument, up there, and Babe must not touch it —' '— *is Easterly 950 feet; Westerly 550 feet; that the total length does not exceed 1500 feet. That the width on the southerly side is 300 feet; that the width on the northerly side is 300 feet; that the end lines are parallel; that the general course of the vein or lode as near as may be is in an Easterly and Westerly direction; that the boundaries of this claim may be readily traced and are defined as follows, to-wit: —!*'"

She skipped a lot of easterly and westerly technique in Casey's clear, uncompromising handwriting — done in an indelible pencil — and came down to the last paragraph:

"'*That all the dips, variations, spurs, angles and all veins, ledges, or deposits within the lines of said claim, together with all water and timber and any other rights appurtenant, allowed by the law of this State or of the United States are hereby claimed.*

LOCATORS
"'*Jack I. Gleason,*
  '*Margaret Sutten.*'

"Why — why-y — Good Lord!"

"Here they come," Casey called at that moment. "Put 'er back in the monument and don't let on like we think they're after this claim at all. It's a darn sight harder to start a fuss when the other fellow don't act like he knows there's any fuss comin'. You ask anybody that ever had a fight."

The Little Woman slowly folded the paper and stood holding it in her hand and staring down at Casey. "But why isn't your name on it, Casey Ryan? Why did you put my name on it?"

"We can argue that out," said Casey cheerfully, "when these callers have went. Say, if that monument ain't got a location notice in it when they get here —"

The Little Woman shut her lips rather tight and climbed up and put the red can back under the top rock of the monument. Then she sat down beside it, planted her elbows on her knees, planted her rounded chin in her two calloused little palms and waited for Lucy Lily and her white man. Casey, I will say, had a flash of intuition. He did not go near the Little Woman, but kept on with his mucking.

He was so very busy, in fact, that he did not seem to hear the two when they rode up, but hurled a shovelful of soft dirt directly under the nose of Lucy Lily's pony, making it duck backward and almost lose its footing.

"Hello," said Lucy Lily calmly, when she had quieted the pony and dismounted. "I think you have found Jim's mine, perhaps. I am glad to meet you again. This —" she indicated the heavy-featured man, "— is my husband. We came to take the gold mine which my uncle gave to me when he

CASEY RYAN 237

died. He makes a will and gave me the gold and so I am going to have it."

"Well," said Casey, leaning his shovel against the side of the cut so that he could wipe the sweat of toil from a cheerful face, "have yuh found it yet?"

Lucy Lily looked at him with that veiled animosity which you will see in the eyes of a pig that is driven into a corner. "I think that this is the mine," she said. "You will have to give it back to me because it is for my husband."

Casey reached for his pocket, and the white man also reached for his and pulled out a gun, just about the time Casey brought forth his trusty plug. Casey bit off a corner and squinted up at the man inquiringly, but he made no remark about the weapon.

"This claim happens to be the Devil's Lantern," he told Lucy Lily carelessly. "It belongs to that lady over there. And her pardner in Vegas. I'm workin' for her." To prove it he picked up the shovel and began throwing out dirt that raised a cloud of dust in the glowering face of Lucy Lily, dimming the brightness of her rouged cheeks.

He was taking a risk,— Casey knew that. But he also knew that the Little Woman had her gun, and was watching these two, and that she was absolutely equal to any emergency that might arise. He knew that she must have heard his statement, for he had purposely raised his voice a tone or two.

They muttered to each other, swinging their horses away from Casey's shoveling. Then they rode on to where the Little Woman sat beside her monument, imperturbably watching their approach. Had those two only known it, they were covered with a rifle from the moment they turned their backs upon Casey; though they might not have seen him if they had looked his way. Casey was back in the cut, resting the Little Woman's rifle upon the broken trunk of a sage bush at the rim. His finger was crooked on the trigger, and he would have shot the instant either of them made a hostile move toward the Little Woman.

She seemed to pay no attention to them beyond answering a question by waving one hand toward the monument. Lucy Lily climbed heavily off her pony, eyed the Little Woman curiously, and walked consciously wide of her as she went to read the notice in the little red can. Lucy Lily seemed distinctly crestfallen when she replaced the can.

"It is the Devil's Lantern Mine, and it's hers," she informed her scowling companion. "And a man I don't know his name. I guess we have made ourselves a hell of trouble for nothing. You come." She remounted, rather clumsily because of her weight, and led the way back down the canyon without a word or a glance toward the two who watched her go. You can't beat an Indian for sublime crudity of manner. Without warning or greeting they come, and when they have finished the errand which brought them, they go, and that settles it.

The Little Woman sat for a long while beside the monument, her chin in her two hands, her face turned away from Casey. Nothing, I believe, worries a man like a woman's silence. Casey looked at her every time he threw a shovel of dirt over the dump, and he thought of her while he picked out the broken rock. Was she mad? Had he hurt her feelings? Did she think, mebby, that he had his nerve, naming the claim the Devil's Lantern without asking her? Or did she think, — what in thunder *did* she think?

Casey made up his mind that he could stand it as long as she could. And immediately he began to feel himself an outcast, a pariah in her sight, a person whom she utterly despised, just as she despised Ole and Joe. He knew why he had done what he did, and he knew that he had been happy in the doing, and couldn't have done anything different if he had tried. Why, hell! Didn't a half-interest belong to Jack, both by custom and agreement? The man who grubstaked always got half. And didn't the Little Woman show him the mine? Would he ever have come over to this particular spot and discovered it, hidden as it was? And since she did show it to him, wasn't it hers by right? How could any man have the nerve not to give her a half-interest? Casey drove his pick viciously into a seam in the rock, when he reached that point in his argument, and then swore because the pick broke.

"An' I wisht you'd show me how'n hell you can make more'n two halves outa anything!" he exclaimed aloud in his distraction.

"You might find the answer to that at the end of your rainbow," the Little Woman's voice answered him with a tender kind of mockery. And there she was, standing within three feet of him, holding Babe by the hand and looking at him with such a shine in her gray eyes!

"Oh, Casey Ryan!" she laughed unsteadily, "I think Lucy Lily went directly to the heart of the matter. I am going to adopt her method." She stopped and looked full at Casey, who was engaged at that moment in scrubbing his face wildly with his blue handkerchief.

"I am going to give the gold to my husband for a wedding present," said the Little Woman.

Casey was not looking at her, and so he swallowed hard over that bald statement. "I — I thought — I didn't know's you had a-any —" he floundered and stuck there, out of breath and out of courage, too.

"I haven't — yet," said the Little Woman very quietly. "Are you — spoken for, Casey Ryan?"

Still, Casey swears that he proposed. He's as proud of it as a hen with young ducks, and I think he would whip any man who had the nerve to hint that Casey had to be cornered first.

He came to me for moral support at the wedding, so I helped Casey buy the ring, helped Casey buy a new outfit of clothes, helped him choose the right tie, by Jove. Casey wanted a blue one with wavy threads of rainbow colors squirming all over it, and I saved him from that, I remember. I remember, too, that Babe had one of her "sad" attacks in the middle of the ceremony, and had to be carried out to the kitchen by the preacher's wife, and given a cookie. I thought sure Casey would need something of the sort himself before he was through. I wish you could have seen his knees buckle when the preacher looked him in the eye and began to intone, " Do you take this woman to be your lawful wedded wife — ? "

Oh, say! Casey will murder me, if he ever reads this (but then, Casey never reads stories; that's why I've told so much of the truth about him). Well, believe it or not, when the preacher finished that do-you-take question, and paused with that solemn air after " So long as you both shall live? " Casey was so up in the air that he threw back his shoulders, tilted his head sidewise belligerently and barked, " You ask anybody if I will or not! "

If you don't believe that, you just ask the Little Woman, or the preacher. No one else heard him, fortunately, the preacher's wife being in the kitchen at the moment with Babe, and coming back only when she was called to sign her name as a witness. I'll bet the preacher told her, though.

That's about all, I think, unless you want to know just how the Devil's Lantern mine panned out. As a matter of fact, I don't know, exactly. You see, I made over my half-interest to Casey and his wife as a wedding present, and Casey, confiding to me his fear that the mine was really just a " pocket " that would not hold up under any extensive working, sold out to a company of promoters for fifty thousand dollars. At the same time he managed to work off the silver claim of the Little Woman's on to the same outfit for something like five thousand, and with all that money to start them housekeeping the Casey Ryan family went straight to the American heaven, California. Los Angeles, to be explicit.

I had a letter from Casey just the other day, in which he boasted of having been pinched twice for speeding since those new and drastic traffic laws went into effect. He's driving a Six, and he says it's blue. But I noticed that " very dark " was written in there, in fine handwriting not at all like Casey's. He's tamed, all right; he must be if he permits his wife to censor his letters to as old a friend as I am.

THE END

Bertha Muzzy Bower, born in Cleveland, Minnesota, in 1871, was the first woman to make a career of writing Western fiction and remains one of the most widely known, having written nearly seventy novels. She became familiar with cowboys and ranch life at sixteen when her family moved to the Big Sandy area of Montana. She was nearly thirty and mother of three before she began writing under the surname of the first of her three husbands. Her first novel, *Chip, of the Flying U*, was initially published as a serial in 1904 and was an immediate success. Bower went on to write more books, fourteen in all, about the Flying U, one of the best being the short story collection, *The Happy Family*. In 1933 she turned to stories set prior to the events described in *Chip, of the Flying U*. *The Whoop-up* actually begins this saga, recounting Chip Bennett's arrival in Montana and at the Flying U. Much of the appeal of this saga is due to Bower's use of humor, the strong sense of loyalty and family depicted among her characters, as well as the authentic quality of her cowboys. She herself was a maverick who experimented with the Western story, introducing modern technologies and raising unusual social concerns—such as aeroplanes in *Skyrider* or divorce in *Lonesome Land*. She was sensitive to the lives of women on the frontier and created some extraordinary female characters, notably in Vada Williams in *The Haunted Hills*, Georgie Howard in *Good Indian*, Helen in *The Bellehelen Mine*, and Mary Allison in *Trouble Rides the Wind*, another early Chip Bennett story. She was also able to write Western novels memorable for the characterization of setting and dramatization of nature, such as *Van Patten* or *The Swallowfork Bulls*.

BARKING & DAGENHAM
001 076 937